INLAWS AND OUTLAWS
AND OTHER STORIES

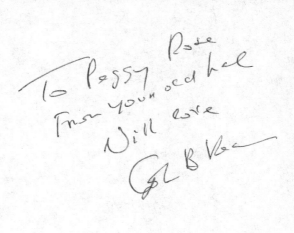

INLAWS

AND

OUTLAWS

AND OTHER STORIES

JOHN B. KEANE

MERCIER PRESS

MERCIER PRESS
PO Box 5, 5 French Church Street, Cork
16 Hume Street, Dublin 2

A CIP record for this book is available from the British Library.

ISBN 1-85635-123-8

10   9   8   7   6   5   4   3   2   1

Printed in Ireland by Colour Books Ltd

CONTENTS

INLAWS AND OUTLAWS

'GIVE ME AN OUTLAW any day before an in-law.' I heard the phrase in the pub one night after a football game during which a number of players had been laid out lovingly on the greensward from right crosses, left hooks and common or garden uppercuts. The man who expressed the opinion quoted at the outset fell foul of an elementary straight left delivered by one of his in-laws.

I disputed his contention at once and asked if in-laws were to be denied the basic right of free-for-all brawling. He hummed and hawed and closed with an unprintable selection of swear words which brings me to the nub of this contribution – the rights of in-laws.

There can be no doubt that most people have a surplus of in-laws with the mother-in-law the main target for revilement, victimisation, misrepresentation and bogus accusations. As an in-law myself I would have to agree that there are in-laws and in-laws and if there is anybody reading this who suffers from a shortage of in-laws let him contact me and I'll gladly supply him with some of mine free of charge. The others I will keep and cherish for the truth is that there is a percentage of blackguards in every denomination under the sun. Police, medics, teachers even clergy have their fair share of bad apples so that if a few turn up on the in-law front we must not be surprised.

I am a man of many in-laws and I would be obliged to concede that only ten per cent or less are troublesome and less than five per cent are truly perverted. Not a bad ratio at all but then I ask myself how can it be explained that there is more bad blood between in-laws than any other form of human relationship?

I think the reason may well be that we take our in-laws for granted and unless we have evening classes on how to deal with in-laws in general the situation will go from bad to worse. We never value anything we take for granted and therefore we don't value our in-laws half enough. We should from this moment onward resolve to make amends for the wrongs we have inflicted on our in-laws and I have no doubt that after a decent interval they will do the same unto us for what is an in-law after all but a semi-detached human with only one gable and very shaky foundations!

What is an in-law in the spiritual sense but a one-winged angel the same as ourselves and what is an in-law in the geographical sense but a victim caught up between two families, neither of his choosing and neither prepared to give in a solitary inch when it matters most!

I remember that the most unfair assessment I ever heard of in-laws as a whole happened one night of Listowel Races many years ago when I wasn't possessed of a solitary grey hair and preferred bull's-eyes to beer.

There was a serious row in progress at the entrance to the marketplace. A man lay on the ground bleeding after being struck by a kettle. The female who inflicted the wound swung the kettle in a wide arc in the hope of adding another casualty to her collection. Mayhem is the only word to describe the awful carnage and screaming and roaring and shouting and pulling and tearing and kicking.

'Get the guards quick!' a man called out, 'before someone is killed.' After a while two guards appeared on the scene. One stood with his back to the market wall while the other went to investigate. Both were elderly chaps, ponderous and easygoing.

The guard who went to investigate succeeded in partially breaking up the row. Slowly he returned to his companion.

'What was that all about?' the companion asked.

'Only in-laws,' came back the weary response.

'You had a right to let them at it,' the other said and with that they disappeared into the night-time together.

THE SMELL OF MONEY

THERE ARE ODOURS THAT touch the heart and others that alert the mind, odours that purify and contaminate, enrich and pauperise and other that linger forever because of happy occasions associated with them.

There is, however, only one odour which, for most people, is the odour of odours, the smell of smells and that my dear readers is the smell of money. Not everybody can pick it up at once. Sometimes it takes long periods before it can be isolated and identified.

Those who can smell it are usually equipped with the means of benefiting from it. Those who cannot are lucky although there are some who would believe that those who cannot smell money are cursed beyond words, have missed the boat in fact. How's that Willie Shakespeare put it 'all the voyage of their life is bound in shallows and in miseries'.

The smell of money is faint, fainter than the gentlest fragrance ever to have been wafted by a breeze. To catch the scent you need a special nose. It need not be a big nose and it does not have to be a small nose. Indeed it does not have to be any kind of nose. I don't have a nose for money. I have been wrong about it all the days of my life and for this I am truly grateful. Nearly all my friends are paupers. There are a few millionaires as worthy and as compassionate as any but at the outset I could not tell the difference between rich and poor.

I have a relative who is different. Let his nose be stuffed by influenza or rendered inoperable by the common cold, it matters not. He can smell money from any given distance, late or early.

Not all people with money give off an odour. They smell just like ourselves. Unfortunately, however, the majority do and there are certain sensitive souls who can smell it with their eyes closed so to speak. I love that phrase 'so to speak'. I cherish it for the number of occasions it has come to my aid. Another benefactor is 'as it were'. Bless them both for the good they have done.

Alas, as is my wont, I digress. Digressions are to me what drawings of breath are to others. Then there was a female neighbour of mine lacking in worldly goods as it were. For many years she was left on the shelf and it seemed that she would never be taken down. Then one day a young man fell off his motorbike as he sped down the street. He seem-ed to be all right and maybe that's why nobody came to his aid, nobody that is, except my female neighbour. He also seemed to be down and out if one was to judge by his apparel but then apparel can be deceiving although Shakespeare, generally right, would have us believe that 'the apparel oft proclaims the man'. Shakespeare was wrong as many a victim who fell foul of a wolf in sheep's clothing will testify.

The man who fell from the motorbike had a face and hands which were tainted with oil and grease. There was also a powerful off-putting body odour which came from being wrapped up so tightly. However underneath the lot was the unmistakable scent of money, weak and barely discernible but instantly recognisable by my neighbour.

She saw to his wants such as steadying him on his feet, wiping the grease from his face and volunteering a chair upon which it was suggested he might sit until his full senses had returned to him. He was quite overcome and we shall never know whether it was due to some derangement caused by his fall or some other factor which made him propose to my neighbour as soon as his balance had asserted itself. She accepted with alacrity as they say but they did not live happily ever after so we may conclude that a nose for money is no great advantage in the long run.

ARSERS

IN MY HEYDAY, MANY moons ago now, great store was set by the size and weight of a man's posterior. Today, unless you're a rugby forward, little store is set by large rumps. In fact it could be said that they are a decided disadvantage when impressing members of the opposite sex is taken into account. I remember when I was a garsún to hear my grand-aunt say of a man who was selected as anchor for a tug of war team 'God knows he has the arse for it even if he has nothing else'. The same lady was a pretty outspoken person and did not mince words when she wanted to make a point.

I recall another occasion when a great lumbering hulk of a fellow paid a visit to a relation's house in the hill country. He drank and ate all round him and would have cleaned out the modest larder entirely if he had been granted access to it. When he went outside to take the air for a spell nobody had a good word to say about him except one old man who couldn't put a hard word on anyone even if he was paid for it.

'What to you think of him Sam?' the woman of the house asked.

'I'll tell you this,' said Sam, 'and that is he has the arse of a mower if he never mowed a sop.'

And so he had and he never did mow a sop for

his only interests in life were eating and drinking unless you call sitting down all day saying and doing nothing an interest.

In the days of the hiring fairs men would be asked to go through their paces in order to determine if they were sound in wind and limb and so forth and so on. Men with big rumps were favoured over men with little rumps and so were often granted better terms although it has been my experience that men with hardly any posteriors to speak of were the liveliest workers of all and never tired because they had to carry so little about.

Indeed it has been my experience that wherever I encountered or witnessed a rabble in action nearly all of its members had outsize posteriors and were only good for pushing from behind where nobody could see them.

The notion that a man with an outsize bum was better began to die when more attention was paid to brain than brawn. Men with excessive arses would always be better at some things than men without but in the last analysis the arse would play second fiddle to the noodle and this was as it should be. The belief that a man with an outsize posterior was steadier on his feet may well have been true but this only applied when he was on terra firma and the higher he climbed the more likely he was to come a cropper.

On the other hand the late and great matchmaker Dan Paddy Andy O'Sullivan had great faith

in men with outsize bottoms. 'Women prefers 'em',
Dan would say in his homely way. What he should
have said was that some women preferred them.
Experts in the field would tell you that it was
shapeliness rather than bulk that most impressed
females who, God bless and spare them, would
never allow themselves to be caught up in such
vulgar argument.

Others believed that a man could not loiter at
will unless he had a large bum. Hence the expression 'arseing around'. They believed that you needed a large behind if you wanted to go arseing
around.

Then there was the occasion when a lady applied for a job on the premises of a friend of mine
who could be quite pointed and succinct when it
suited her. We asked her after some time how the
new employee was working out.

'She's an arser,' came the ready answer and we
all knew at once what was meant.

PAST INCISIONS

OH THE KINDNESS OF people plain and otherwise! As I recover from recent operations I am overwhelmed by greetings of goodwill. I am once again reminded of the innate goodness of men and women, of their concern for others and their compassion and also, of course, the great urges of a substantial minority who waylay the likes of myself with queries about my health without waiting for an answer.

Instead they regale themselves with accounts of operations they have had themselves and I am forced to submit my unwilling ears to long, lonesome accounts of past incisions, severance's, lacerations and avulsions.

For the most part I listen for basically these are kind people who really suffer from no more than an exaggerated sense of their own surgical importance. They need audiences the way an open wound needs stitches so I feel impelled to stand my ground and hear them out. I mean where's the point in undergoing a serious operation if you can't boast about it now and then.

The problem arises when the weather is inclement and there seems to be very little weather of any other kind in recent times. There I was a week ago walking back Market Street in my native town. From all sides messages of goodwill assailed my ears. The rain came down and consequently the greetings and acknowledgements were of the briefest duration until I was seized by one particular gentleman who bore a small umbrella which barely covered his head, his head mark you, not our heads.

He shook my hand and asked me how I was. I told him but he heeded me not. Instead he went into a long and detailed account of his prostate operation. All the time he held me firmly with one hand while the other was used to hold the umbrella over his head.

In vain I looked around for an avenue of escape and when I found none I fervently prayed that some passer-by would interrupt and ask me how I was feeling. Nothing happened.

I tried to tear myself away but I lacked the strength which I took for granted before my operation.

'I have to be going!' I called out but there was no loosening of the vice-like grip. This predator of shuffling convalescents had a tale to tell and he was going to tell it.

The Ancient Mariner had nothing on him as he tightened his grip and drew his umbrella closer to his head oblivious of my bared cranium bombarded by wind and rain. By this stage he was running through the family history of the surgeon who had performed the operation.

'I have to go,' I shouted and tugged with all my rapidly diminishing strength. All to no avail as he informed me that the surgeon's son had also gone into medicine and was doing well for himself, having married well to boot, and having an even nicer manner than the father. Again I looked around in vain and then I realised exactly where I was. I was standing outside the public toilet, that most approachable benefactor of bladder and bowel, often maligned and ignored by the snobbish and the continent. Have you ever heard of a politician officially opening a public toilet! Have you ever heard of a queen or a princess or an ecclesiastical dignitary consenting to perform such a task!

'The toilet,' I cried out in anguish and with a superhuman effort made a dash to its recesses, closing the door in my wake.

I could hear him from a distance still pattering on about the number of stitches that had been inserted for another operation which had been performed on him many years before. I waited until his voice turned hoarse and was finally no more than a whisper. Then I made my move. Girding my loins and rebuttoning my trousers I dashed forth into the wind and the rain and had crossed the road before he had a chance to obstruct me.

There were other similar encounters after which I resolved to skirt the town's streets and opt for its quieter suburbs and surrounds. How vain and how foolish are we who believe that trouble can be circumvented by a mere change of location! Trouble my dear readers is everywhere. We are all in this world to bear our share of it and we must not be surprised when those who inflict it appear suddenly as though out of nowhere.

I was to enjoy a few peaceful days after my ordeal outside the public toilet in Market Street.

Listowel is possessed of many fine byways and backways as well as leafy lanes and abundant parklands and it was to these I turned for my daily exercises. Enquiries about my health were gentle and brief and concerned and my well-wishers listened attentively while I hastily defined the exact stage of my recuperation.

I was asked about my appetite, my bowels, my sleep and what-have-you but all in the most discreet form imaginable and all by the most concerned and humane of individuals.

Then one day as I reached the upper end of Church Street, that majestic thoroughfare where I first saw the light, I found my pathway blocked by an elderly gentleman with a long tale to tell. He linked his arm with mine giving the impression that his motives were purely safeguarding. To look at his face you would quite honestly believe that a harrowing account of a bygone operation was the last thing in his head. I must say that up until this time I did not really believe that the dead came to the aid of the living but as you shall see gentle reader the dead did.

My new tormentor then released his hold. He merely blocked my progress every time I tried to pass by. It transpired that he once had an operation for information of the bowel, at least that's what he called it.

He took me through the ordeal step by step until I grew so weak that I felt I must surely disintegrate in a heap at his feet. Again my surroundings came to my aid for there by my side was the gate which leads into the graveyard. I love graveyards. No harm will come to you there and we may pray for our beloved departed in the balmy confines. You'll never see a bad word about anyone in a graveyard. Sweet graveyard, great repository of monumental hyperbole! I excused myself on the grounds that I had to pray for the dead, that I hadn't done so since I took ill. I was gone in a flash and prayed for all those who had come to my aid.

A PRODIGY

THE PIECE DE RESISTANCE of a visit to some recently-acquired acquaintances was the introduction of their two-year-old prodigy who, at his parents' request, effed and blinded like a chap twice his age.

Ah how the times have changed! In my childhood parents would take pride in the fact that a child could say his prayers or even sing a song for the titillation of visitors.

After the two-year-old prodigy had finished his rendition our acquaintances were astonished that we did not respond with a standing ovation. My wife, the most tactful of creatures, felt constrained to tender a minor criticism.

'They're all at it these days,' she said at which the mother of the toddler with considerable vehemence exclaimed that she knew of children in their third and even fourth years who couldn't curse at all, at all.

My spouse, of course, as usual was right. There's hardly a child in the country who hasn't acquired a certain proficiency for effing and blinding and there are many who are veritable virtuosos, often astounding their own parents hitherto unaware of the geniuses in their midst.

At this stage I would like to inform the parents

A PRODIGY

and relations of these under-age marvels that I am
not criticising. Rather am I an observer who records
the changes in society as he knows it for the spiritual and intellectual advancement of his readers.

I have been present at gatherings where a three-
year-old confounded and shocked his listeners with
an elementary tirade consisting of two or three
words repeated ad nauseam. I have also heard onlookers scoff at the best efforts of the effers-and-
blinders in question and announce in asides to
whoever might be at hand that their own offspring
would leave the so-called entertainers in the shade.

'You should hear our Charlie,' I heard a female
say to a group of listeners who had just been subjected to a stirring performance by a toddler who
would not obey his mother's injunction to refrain
from piddling on the floor of the supermarket
where the action was taking place.

'No,' said her partner, 'Kate is better. She can
eff and blind at twice the rate.'

There's an elderly gentleman who frequents
these premises on a regular basis. He is a chaste individual who fought in two major wars and travelled the world in his spare time.

'I have never heard of the likes,' he announced
one evening as he listened to a brother and sister of
three and four respectively effing and blinding each
other and indulging too in more uncommon swear
words.

'I have been all over the world,' he said, 'and I

once resided in a small flat between two brothels although I was never part of a horizontal pairing, and I never heard the likes of what I heard here today from these children.'

'You should hear them coming from school!' a middle-aged gin and tonic informed him, 'they'd make the hair stand on your head.'

The worst I have personally heard emanated from the mouth of a two-year-old whose mother had just refused him her breast as part of a continuing effort to wean him off it altogether. I was badly rattled after his outpourings but fair play to his gallant mother she did not give in to his demands. You're right! She told him to eff off for himself.

No Chairs

I FONDLY RECALL AN old lady who lived a few doors down the street from the house where I was born. At the front of the house was a small shop which her husband tended all day long. Behind the shop was a small kitchen. There was no other room downstairs. She had a great method of dealing with unwanted visitors.

She would remove all the chairs in the kitchen to the backyard at the sight of known interlopers. All were welcome to call but she had been held hostage all too often in the past by those who over-stayed their leave.

I was often party to her subterfuges and once when a large party of rustic relations appeared in the shop we lifted the kitchen table which had just been laid for supper out into the backyard. This was followed by the chairs and by a small stool. These would have been the total seating arrange-ments of the kitchen.

When unwelcome squatters arrived the first thing they did was to try and find a place where they could sit down. Upon finding none they were generally too polite to comment on the absence of chairs. When somebody did ask a direct question about them she had stock replies at the ready.

'Oh,' she would say, 'I'm after washing them

and they won't be dry for a while.'

Other times she would say that they were being painted and if certain more resolute arrivals intimated they were going to hang around anyway she would point out that the chairs had been removed to facilitate washing of the kitchen floor. There is absolutely no comfort to be found in a kitchen where the floor is being scrubbed.

One would think that these actions altogether would deter the unwelcome visitor. Far from it. They would endeavour to surprise her by suddenly seeking entry but, as always, the kitchen door was bolted and could only be opened from the inside. She had, of course, a few chosen friends. I was one of these and could sit at will although, to tell the truth, young chaps of my age and gender rarely spent more than a few minutes in the same place.

The idea often occurred to me that long tedious meetings might easily be subverted by having all chairs removed beforehand. All the participants would be forced to stand regardless of their sex or size and in this way the meeting would come to an end at a reasonable hour. In my early days or nights at meetings there were no distractions on offer. There was no television and very few had motor cars. There was no free travel and there were no community centres so what could be more inviting, I ask you, than a nice warm room with plenty of chairs where one could pass the night in non-contributory comatoseness. The longer the meeting the better, for it cost the members nothing and there was no cheaper way of passing a long, winter's night.

In the rural Ireland of the time the annual general meeting was a diversion second only to the annual visit of the missionaries but while the missionary confinement lasted only an hour the proceedings at the general meeting could and did go on all night.

I would respectfully suggest to people who are obliged to tend meetings to ensure early termination by the simple expedient of removing all the chairs beforehand. It's the only known method of circumventing large, ponderous bores and there's no better antidote for curbing compulsive talkers. Inevitably somebody is bound to ask why there are no chairs but this can be neatly included under Any Other Business or if the chairman is tough enough he can rule the question is out of order.

A NIGHT TO REMEMBER

DID I EVER TELL you about the time my father risked his life for his family and his neighbours! It was pay day 1933, the first or second day in November to be exact. He was paid monthly like all teachers at the time. As usual in the pub that night he had one too many. He always did on the nights of pay days.

Accompanying him was a stalwart neighbour who shared in his good fortune. We shall call him Jack. As was their wont they entered our house by the backway but the moment they stepped inside the back gate they were assaulted by several men wearing white garments. A fierce fight ensued in which no quarter was asked or given.

It lasted a full hour during which not a single utterance escaped the mouths of the men in the white sheets. At first my father thought it might be the Ku Klux Klan but during the engagement he asked himself why the dreaded southerners would make such a long journey just to attack a middle-aged schoolteacher and his elderly friend.

Eventually the fight ended and the assailants fled leaving behind them their white garments.

In the kitchen of our house my father and his

friend saw to their wounds. They congratulated themselves on their courage. Of the two Jack had suffered the more. He had a loose tooth and a black eye whereas my father was lucky enough to escape with scratches and minor abrasions. The commotion had awakened every member of the family. Some brandy which was reserved for medicinal purposes was produced. My father and Jack finished it off in no time at all and sat themselves wearily down while they tried to identify their assailants. My mother asked if they might have been from the other world, members of the banshee family or even the Puca but my father was convinced the creatures were human, 'for,' said he, 'I struck one of the scoundrels twice and I heard him grunt the same way as a human might under the circumstances.'

'They were humans all right,' his friend Jack concurred. 'The chap who struck me smelled of strong drink and he also called me a wretch.'

At this stage the girl who worked in the house entered the kitchen. She was, we all knew, governed by full moons and would watch a full moon all night long until the stars faded from the heavens. She had seen the invaders from an upstairs window and yet she wasn't distraught or incoherent or anything like that. In fact she seemed to find it difficult to hold back the laughter. We thought she was on the verge of a bout of hysteria. The moon had affected her thus at least once in the past. All she could do was point at my father and his friend and hold her laughter at bay.

This annoyed my father no end. Was it for this he and his friend had risked their lives!

'Speak up woman,' he commanded curtly, 'tell us what you saw. Were they human or were they supernatural?'

'They were sheets,' she responded with a smile, 'the sheets on the washing line.'

'But who struck me?' Jack asked.

'Himself,' said the girl. She always referred to my father as himself. 'Himself struck you when the sheet was wrapped around your head. He said you were a wretch.'

'But,' my father expostulated, 'where did I get all these scratches and abrasions?'

'Clothes pegs,' the girl explained. 'When the wind whipped off the sheets the clothes pegs hit you.'

There followed a long silence. All of us, save my mother, crawled back upstairs to our beds. Later that night after Jack had gone home my mother told my father she was proud of him.

'I know what it's like,' she said, 'to get a slap of a wet sheet, yet you faced a line full of them thinking they were out to get your family and your wife. What you did was heroic and I'm honoured to be married to you.'

SPUD-PEELING

THE FIRST SEMINAR WHICH I ever attended was directed by my late, beloved mother. It was one of the more important of many which I attended throughout the course of a lifetime almost.

It might never have taken place had not we been left to our own devices during a dinnertime when both parents were unavoidably elsewhere. When they returned they fell foul of misplaced potato skins which had fallen to the floor during the course of the meal. My mother rose immediately to her feet whereas my father was incapacitated for several days and had a visit from the doctor and all because we, his offspring, made a mess of peeling our potatoes.

There was no retribution for two reasons. The first was that my father, because of the injury to his back, was incapable of inflicting punishment and the second was that my mother's attention was diverted solely to her husband after his collapse.

Then came Christmas or rather Christmas Eve. A large pot of spuds had been boiled after the supper and would be peeled before being mashed for potato stuffing as soon as my mother got around to it.

On this occasion we were made to gather round the kitchen table while she peeled the first, second and third spuds. The first was a rather small spud. She lofted it on to a fork and peeled it with great skill and efficiency. The second was a medium sized spud. It received the same treatment as the first except that the process was slower lest it disintegrate on the prongs of the fork. The third spud was a very large tuber and this she cut in half before pronging both halves separately and then peeling them.

She then bade us be seated and played a supervisory role while we peeled the remainder of the spuds. Mashing was a mere formality. It was a job which should not be rushed, however, lest lumpy mash be the result.

'Wherever you are,' my mother said afterwards, 'don't ever be ashamed to pull up your sleeves if you're peeling dicey spuds,' i.e., spuds that were too large or too floury or too cumbersome to rest steadily while impaled on the fork prongs. What a lovely word is prong!

> Prong along with me for Christmas
> Prong along with me my dear,
> Then we'll mash and bash the peeled potatoes
> And have a Christmas full of cheer.

So we see gentle reader how important it is to peel our spuds properly. Before we may peel however we have to prong, meaning to impale the spud so that it will not fall apart. Here is where so many spud peelers get it all wrong. If the spud is too small it will split and if it is too large it will not sit steadily on the prongs. I have seen clergymen and doctors as well as musicians and schoolmasters who could not properly peel spuds. This may well be because during their young years their spuds were peeled for them by loving mothers.

The efficient peeling of spuds is a rare accomplishment while it must also be said that a man who makes a mess of peeling his spud may well make a mess of everything else.

When I was younger I went with a friend to a well-known hotel where he sought out the manager with a view to booking the premises for his sister's wedding breakfast. Very kindly the manager who happened to be lunching at the time invited us to join him at the table. He was in the process of peeling a rather large, floury potato. When it disintegrated, as my friend and I knew it must, my friend excused himself indicating that I should follow him. Outside, he shook his head.

'A good job we caught him in the act,' he said, 'if the fellow cannot be trusted to peel his own spud imagine the mess he'd make of a wedding breakfast!' Peel your spuds with care then and be seen to be peeling them with care. *In hoc signo vinces, amen.*

HAPPY TIMES

MANY YEARS AGO A friend of mine took a girl to
Ballybunion for the day. They travelled by bus for
in those distant days few had cars. They strolled
along the beach and without warning he suddenly
seized her hand and held on to it as though it were
a lifebuoy.

They had not known each other long and when
he proposed, a week or so before, that they spend a
day by the sea she suggested Ballybunion and so it
was that they found themselves strolling along the
dark brown strand or the golden strand as some
call it. What does the song say:

> Though my feet are planted in a far-off land
> There is somewhere else they'd rather be,
> Faith 'tis planted firmly in the deep brown sand
> Where the Shannon River meets the sea.

Anyway, there they were savouring the champagne
air for which this romantic resort is justly famed
when the tenderest of physical notions assailed
him. Quite carried away or should I say swept
away by the cries of the gulls, the blue of the skies
and the gentle lapping of the often thunderous
Atlantic waves he flung his arms around her and
kissed her flush on the lips. She neither cried nor
sighed nor could it be said that she in the least way

denied him. They resumed their walking without further resorting to romantic overtures. Then uptown they went where he plied her with cold mutton, tomatoes, brown bread and scalding tea. They rambled round and about flitting from the Castle Green to the caves of Doon and from Mikey Joe's Irish-American Bar to the Black Rocks and back again.

When the first, faint stars appeared they headed for the Pavilion Ballroom where they danced for over three hours to the music of Pat Crowley's inimitable orchestra. Then they went homeward, aided and abetted by a neighbour who obliged them with a lift.

The happy tale concludes here. Perhaps I should say that they later married, had children and lived happily ever after, or relatively so, when they weren't scolding each other.

What is the purpose of all this, what is the moral, the sub-story, the message! There are none. The man in question merely related the happy occasion to a group of friends who happened to be gathered in these here licensed premises at the time. Each member of the party was remembering in turn the happiest day of his or her life. When our friend had finished a lady dabbed at her eyes with a mini-handkerchief while another asked if the mutton had been tender. If there is anything to be drawn from remembrance of that happy day it is that we should take a backward look occasionally and refresh ourselves from the wells of happiness which are still partly-filled from those halcyon days. How does the song say:

This is my lovely day,
This is the day I shall remember
The day I'm dying ...

And so it goes on. There is no amusement tax payable on these happy memories and we need these bright backward glances to sustain us in the blacker days that all too often abound.

One of the party when asked to recall her happiest day announced that it was the day her husband expired. He was, she explained, fond of drawing a clout at her and even a kick if the drink made him playful. He never gave her any money and never took her anywhere.

'I was delirious with joy when he passed on,' she continued, 'and even more delirious to learn from his lawyer that he had spent only a fraction of his money.'

So you see gentle reader all is not lost. You may recall the happiest of times in the midst of unpleasant ones.

PURSES

SOME TIME AGO I wrote about the advantages of excuse-me dances and how they saved many a bruised female toe from further destruction. All a suffering girl had to do was cast her eyes heavenwards during an excuse-me and succour would be instantly forthcoming from the headlands of the dance hall in the shape of a young man who knew when a lady was in distress.

Now we will look at the female purse in relation to the common or garden dance and we will list a number of the countless accessories which such a purse might hold if the contents were catalogued at any given dance.

Apart altogether from containing the accoutrements of beautification among other things the purse was also used as a deposit on a young man. Let me elaborate.

Should a young lady cast her eye on a young man to whom she found herself attracted and should she wish to sustain his interest without fully committing herself she would ask him to mind her purse until the dance was over.

In this way she was intimating that she would be available at the end of the proceedings should he put his name forward as an escort to her home, her bicycle or her car. It was often a highly successful method of establishing a meaningful relationship which might or might not lead to the altar.

It was also possible for a young lady to change her mind over the course of the dancing and demand her purse back on the grounds that she had to go home early or go home with a friend or sister. These were the more painless methods of dispossessing the unfortunate hopeful who thought that he was on the pig's back upon being handed the purse in the first place.

There were certain young ladies however who carried two purses, one of which was worthless and would contain nothing at all, except maybe a tattered handkerchief.

The other purse which was the genuine article would contain her lipstick, her compact with inbuilt mirror and pancake make-up, her money limited and all that it might be, her mascara, house keys, rosary beads, hair clips, combs and hankies to mention but some of the articles common to the female purse of the period, Oh dear me, I forgot perfume, the *sine qua non*, without which a girl was as powerless as a highwayman who had forgotten his pistol.

Having deposited the empty purse she was assured at least of the attentions sooner or later of a relatively acceptable young man who would almost certainly suggest that he was the very person to escort her to her abode wherever that might be.

Then of course should she change her mind

during the run of the dance there was always the real thing. She would be genuinely attracted to the young man who would be favoured with the genuine article so that it was imperative she keep it in reserve until she was prepared to make her final choice.

She need not search out the unfortunate chap with the worthless article and maybe hurt his feelings. Why break his heart when he might go home and dream of what might have been!

We see then that the experienced young lady would not make an immediate choice or, to put it another way, place all her eggs in one basket. Rather would she feel her way with the worthless purse in the hope that something better might show up. Unlike proportional representation her second preference was more valuable than her first.

There were scoundrels too who would abscond with a purse for the sake of its monetary contents but this was a rare occurrence and most young men would rather die than do such a thing.

Oddly enough there are no songs about purses and how I long for a song that might begin, 'Throw me your purse from across the room ...'

THE REAL MORAL

WE HAD A CHAP in the extended family one time who endeavoured to make fun out of everything. The bother lay in the fact that what was fun to him was quite painful to others. I remember the day his aunt got the fit. The news was broken to him on the street by a relative.

'Your aunt is after taking a turn for the worse,' he was told.

'Was it a right or a left hand turn?' he quipped. When the relative upbraided him he apologised on the ground that he misunderstood.

'Well you know the kind of turn I mean,' the relative put in hotly. Now it transpired that the aunt in question was a great warrant to feed birds. When in the city she would purchase a pan loaf and disburse it among the ducks and coots of St Stephen's Green. At the seaside she would feed seabirds.

'Was it,' asked the quipper, 'a common Tern she took or an Arctic Tern?'

When no answer was forthcoming he announced that he knew it would happen sooner or later.

'A Tern!' he mused, 'I always thought she'd take a Duck. She was closer to Ducks.'

When he arrived home the first thing he did

was change his socks.

'Your aunt is failing,' his mother advised him.

'So what!' he responded, 'I failed in my time and look at me now. I have several pairs of high quality socks. I failed my Inter and Leaving and I even failed the breathalyser but that's all behind me.'

So saying he tied his laces, attached his clips and went for a cycle. His mother shook her head. All she could say was, 'the supper will be on the table in half an hour.'

At the cross-roads outside the town he was hailed by a passing policeman who informed him that his aunt was waning.

'Wain, wain go to Spain,' he said and left a puzzled policeman in his wake. Thrice he cycled round the town in an effort to work up an appetite for his supper. Thrice the same news assailed his ears.

'Your aunt is gone into a coma,' said a sympathetic shopkeeper who chanced to be sweeping the street in front of his premises.

'She never goes near Acoma,' he threw back and in this he was correct for his aunt despised the neighbouring village of Acoma and its inhabitants. She had been jilted by an Acoma shoemaker in her late twenties and as a result could not look upon lasts, awls, wax cord or heel-ball.

'Your aunt is going down,' a friend of his mother's called as he changed gears going up an incline.

'So is the price of butter,' he called back.

'Your aunt is dying,' shouted a neighbouring publican.

'Is it her coat or her hair?' he asked as he mounted the footpath before executing a neat turn-about. He pedalled down the slope without a care in the world and in doing so he managed to beat his aunt to the punch.

He ran straight into a bus. Rumour had it that his eyes were shut at the time but as he might put it himself, 'it will spare the mortician the bother of closing them.'

All very fine, the gentle reader will say but where is the moral? I could say that mocking is catching and get away with it. I could also say that one should never drive while one's eyes are closed. It would be a valid moral. The real moral is, of course, that he should have had a bottle of stout before his supper and not cycle round the town provoking God and man. *Quod semper, quod ubique, quod ab omnibus.*

WHO ARE WE!

MANY YEARS AGO THERE was a man who walked around the outskirts of this town every day. He never ventured into the heart of the town nor, indeed, to its immediate suburbs. He lived in a small house about two miles from the town centre. Some said that there was a woman in the house and some said there was not.

It was believed that he was in receipt of a small pension from the United States where he had spent thirty-five of his seventy odd years. Certainly the postman called to the house once a week but his lips were sealed as is the wont of postmen everywhere when quizzed about their deliveries.

We will call our friend who traversed the outer suburbs by the name of Xerxes. The first time I came across him was on the bend of a narrow goat-path. He motioned me to silence and pointed to a broader passage, clearly visible through the scant, slender reeds which surrounded us. I was quite young at the time.

'Pheasant,' he said, 'and her brood.'

Sure enough a hen pheasant picked her way daintily westwards followed by seven chicks. We watched until they disappeared from view. Excitedly he began to babble. There were several other broods which came and went at all hours of the day and there were nests of mallard secreted by hidden streams overhung by fern and meadow-sweet and blistering nettle.

I was amazed at the amount he knew. I accompanied him westwards. I had heard wise men say that he knew nothing.

'I mean,' one man opined, 'how could he know anything when he goes nowhere and sees nothing!' We walked towards a small grove of black alder. As we neared it a hare broke from heavy cover in its midst and took off in what seemed like a leisurely fashion. In reality he moved at great speed. Hares are deceptively fast. It is their grace and loping style that makes them look indolent.

My friend did not comment on the hare's departure. He raised a finger to his lips and indicated that there might well be young hares in a nest nearby.

The second time we met and the last time was very near the same spot where first I encountered him, I was much older. We spoke of the weather. Then when we smelled tobacco smoke in the wind he bade me to follow him. Through a clump of whins he pointed to a woman who stood silently in the deserted roadway. She was smoking a cigarette. She savoured every powerful drag as though it were about to be her last. I knew her well. She was a beautiful woman if her youth was behind her itself.

'Husband won't let her smoke,' Xerxes informed me. We moved westwards. Suddenly he paused like a pointer and indicated a man in the distance who squatted as he relieved himself in the great outdoors.

'Can't do it indoors,' Xerxes informed me, 'comes here all the time. Spends ages at it. Often talks away to himself.' We moved off towards the twilight. He pointed out many interesting features of the landscape as the sun sank, leaving a roseate glow in the far heavens.

'It's beautiful,' he said and then he pointed to a man who chanced to be knocking at the door of an isolated house. A woman answered and swiftly, stealthily he entered. She closed the door but not before she looked up and down the narrow road-way.

'See,' said Xerxes, 'how paragons perform when the dark is due.'

I nodded that I fully understood, that it was part and parcel of the world.

'No blame,' he said, 'who are we to blame!'

'Who are we!' I echoed. I never met him again. Even his memory is now erased from the minds of those who knew him. The moral is that those who are supposed to know nothing often know most and, knowing most, they understand the most and carry a profound understanding of mankind and other creatures in their minds.

MAN-WHO-SIT-WITH-SIN

MAN-WHO-SIT-WITH-SIN. That was what we called him. These were the kind of names we heard in the cinema when I was a boy. Indian films and Indian talk were all the rage. Man-Who-Sit-With-Sin was so-called because he was hired at Christmas and Easter by the town's overworked businessmen to hold a place on the benches outside the confessionals in St Mary's. He would sit there, often for hours, until the businessman found time to shrive himself. Man-Who-Sit-With-Sin must have known a lot about the morals of his native town but if he did he kept his mind to himself.

Then there was Chief-Who-Thought-Dev-Was-God. He was high up in Fianna Fáil and deified his leader throughout his life.

Then there was Warpaint-On-Toes. She was a young woman fresh from the city whose husband had taken up employment in the town. Warpaint-On-Toes was a really nice lady and I would hate to repeat what was sometimes said about her because she dared to paint her toes and wear slacks.

Then there were the self-evident names like Man-Who-Sing-Like-Dog. This was one of our better ones because he sang like nothing else, especially when he staggered home drunk on Saturday and Sunday nights. Other dogs answered but I would be doing an injustice to the man if I said that he didn't hold his own. Eventually he became more dog than the dogs themselves and it was impossible to distinguish between Man-Who-Sing-Like-Dog and the real dogs of the neighbourhood when the moon was full and the ragged clouds pursued each other across the pale heavens.

Then there was Man-Who-Talks-To-Guards. He will be familiar to most older readers. Every town boasted a man who talked to guards. He never provided the authorities with information or anything like that but whenever he beheld a stationary policeman he couldn't resist the urge to approach him and open a conversation with him.

Man-Who-Talks-To-Guards firmly believed that his status improved from being seen with the boys in blue. Perhaps he secretly dreamed of becoming a civic guard one day.

Some of the names that needed no further explanation were given to people who would never know they were so called. They were in the main, non-communicators and never trusted neighbours or acquaintances with a confidence. Consequently they received none.

There were:

Squaw-With-The-Big-Wind
Big-Chief-Cave-In-The-Face

Big-Chief-Running-Nose
Squaw-With-Eyes-In-Arse
Little-Drunk-Chief-Who-Breaks-Windows
Chief-Who-Chase-Widows
Man-Who-Puke-All-He-Drink
Man-Who-Like-Man

and so forth and so on. The scriptwriters responsible for the names in the Indian films we saw in those far-off days didn't have any edge on us.

There was Chief-Who-Speak-With-Forked-Nose. His nose had been broken in a fight and he spoke partially through that damaged organ.

There was Little-Chief-Who-Spare-Paper. When first I heard this one I foolishly presumed it was given to a man who liked to keep his newspaper until night but how wrong I was.

Little-Chief-Who-Spare-Paper was merely a man who liked to relieve himself out-of-doors and would avail himself, at the completion of such necessary chores, of adjacent dock leaves and grasses in order to complete his toilet. It was a commonplace occurrence although regular outdoor relievers were rare.

There are no such nicknames applied these days. We are too much taken up with other things. We seem to have lost the capacity to create our own amusement.

SMALL FIELDS

THERE'S AN AGRICULTURAL CANNIBALISM afoot these days and it's become so bad that we have started to run out of small fields. Most of them have already been eaten by larger ones and they're not making small ones anymore. The larger ones had better look out too or they'll suffer the same fate.

Small fields with their attendant hedgerows and balm-inducing rivulets were treasure troves of crab trees, thorn black and white, rich in sloe and haw. There was sally, ash and willow and oh the abundance of songbirds chanting, chirping, trilling all through the length of the day!

And what of the morning! Morning time in a small field is surely a corner of paradise with the song of lark and linnet and long-tailed tit and every other that ever did flit. And pray what are the songs they sing! These are the songs they sing; Oh man of the small field and the high hedgerow hang in there for as sure as there's down on the breast of a goose your turn will come again. Your day will dawn when men grow tired of expanding as sure as ducks quack and frogs croak.

Large fields are fine and without them we might starve but we'll have to leave room for little fields or we'll start to lose our identities.

Behind the house where I was born is a small

field. They used to call it the major's field. It was once owned by a retired British army major and after he died we would hear the thunder of horses' hooves during the dead of night. We never looked to see if the major was spurring his mount as they raced towards the dawning of day but you can be sure he was and that's why we never looked. The field is still there but the hoof beats have long since gone. There are horses still to be seen there but they don't thunder after dark because these are horses of flesh and blood whereas the major's was a horse of the mind and I daresay the arrival of the electric light had a hand in his eclipse as it did with the pooca and the headless coach and Jack o' the Lantern.

Yes there is agricultural cannibalism abroad and it's time we shouted stop. Some men look at a small field and they see it as part of a larger field. Others look at it and they see a building site but every time I see a small field I see a sanctuary. Here I may be serenaded and here I may rest or even sleep nights in summertime.

Men may shake their heads and say that the small field is gone forever but I say no. I have too much faith in men who still own small fields and remember that men who have large fields have small fields too, one often complimenting the other. Remember Latvia and Albania and Lithuania. Were they not cannibalised too in their time! Look at them now, rampant and upsurging and independent again. Let us not give up on our smaller fields. There is a place for them in the patchwork quilt of agriculture.

The small field is distinctive. It has its own smell, easily recognisable, often dominated by woodbine or muskrose, other times by clovers or by odours freed when green grass is crushed or by the scent of newly cut hay and silage or by the wild blooms of summertime or by the gentle decay of winter. The odours are wafted away by the breezes in the larger fields but the smaller fields with their protective whitethorns and blackthorns and sundry small trees retain the fragrance that makes them individual.

Remember too that a small sheltered field is a great place to recline at leisure when the head throbs after an unsuccessful lunch. One may nod and doze far from the maddening crowd until the drowsiness is vanquished by the sublime slumber that only a small sheltered field can induce. The excesses of the night before become more memories and, before long, an appetite for supper is born.

Just like ourselves there are no two small fields alike but there is, alas, a sameness to larger pastures, good in themselves but let us also have the fulsome flavour of the smaller so that we might cherish our own distinctiveness.

SEEING THINGS

AND NOW, A WORD or two about seeing things. I draw upon the sean-fhocal, one swallow doesn't make a summer or, if you like, one kiss does not make a romance.

Anyway to proceed and to begin with as the song says, my mother and I were once walking through the grove of Gurtenard in my native town when our ears were unexpectedly assailed by female laughter. It brightened the woodlands and flushed a drowsy blackbird from his arboreal hideaway. He was a fine bird and he was very annoyed if one was to believe his protestations.

We came upon the girls as they sauntered happily and blithely without a care in the world at that particular time. Care never leaves us alone for long and will return to pester us no matter how high we climb the ladder of ecstasy.

Unaware of our presence the girls stood stock still for a moment, embraced gently and kissed. I was roughly ten years of age at the time but young as I was it had come to my ears that there were girls who kissed each other on a regular basis. It was a far less enlightened climate than now.

'Look,' I said to my mother, 'two girls kissing.' She nodded, having already noted the situation. She sauntered onwards without speaking. I was surprised because she had always been prepared to comment on anything and everything. Then the girls disappeared from view around a bend. My mother paused.

'Could be,' she said matter-of-factly, 'that they are learning how to kiss and must practice with each other for the want of a boyfriend. That way they'll be ready when a boyfriend comes along.'

For the time and place it was a good answer. I never saw those girls again but I have a feeling they are happy somewhere.

Then there was the Sunday afternoon my father and I went walking in the same area. It was wintertime and birds were scarce on the ground and in the air. There was a deep silence in the grove due to the absence of a breeze. Then there was some shouting and the sound of running footsteps. We paused and beheld two young men, one wearing goggles and the other a leather visor.

'Where are their motor bikes?' I asked my father.

'They are not bikers,' my father informed me. I remember having pressed him for an answer of some kind.

'They are rugby players,' he explained. I let it go at that. Something in the trees overhead distracted me. Maybe it was the beginning of a breeze. It would be some time before I fully comprehended why rugby players would be wearing goggles and visors. It did not happen really until I found myself in a similar predicament. The goggles and visor were disguises. If the young men in question had been identified they would undoubtedly be suspended from playing Gaelic football for such was the law of the time that if a Gaelic footballer played rugby or attended a rugby dance he would be suspended by his club from playing the native games. There were extreme feelings in the air at the time and, when certain things are in the air, issues get clouded. Vision gets clouded as well.

So we see how easy it is to be mistaken and how simple it is to deduce wrong impressions. We see too how things change with the passage of time and how today's virtue was often yesterday's transgression.

DRAWING A BLANK

ONE OF THE MORE intimidating experiences to which I have all too often been subjected is to be confronted by a blank sheet of foolscap on the morning after a wedding or indeed any outing where the consumption of intoxicating drink is involved.

Surely, the more experienced reader will say that by not indulging in intoxicating drink the problem would not present itself and the filling of blank pages with readable material would be no problem.

Nobody knows this better than I do. Even before I set out on the drinking foray I already know the consequences. The burned child they say dreads the fire but, alas, this does not mean that the debilitated hangover victim dreads the drink. I should know better but unfortunately I don't.

Staring at a blank page is like looking at a murky sky waiting for the incessant rain to stop. It's akin to asking a miser for money, to ploughing with a rubber plough, to go fishing with no hook on your line, to shaving with no blade in your razor or to combing your hair with a comb that has no teeth.

How often in the past have I sat over the better part of an afternoon looking at the blank page.

Worse still how many blank pages have I rendered useless with beginnings that were never really going anywhere.

There are psychologists who would advise writers that the best thing to do is go away and leave the empty page alone. Let it lie fallow and come back to it another time. A colleague once told me that he made twenty-two starts at a story in one day and wound up consigning twenty-two defaced and crumpled sheets of foolscap to the wastepaper basket.

I have never gone that far but there have been occasions when I have rolled up as many as six or even seven sheets and dumped them in sheer desperation. It wouldn't be so bad if one didn't have a deadline. Instead of being the spur the deadline fulfils a role which is the very opposite. The more one's deadline diminishes the less likelihood is there of anything worthwhile appearing on the page. Never, therefore, trust yourself to a deadline. Whatever chance at all you might have without a deadline there is no earthly chance with one. Oh sure! You'll knock off a thousand words but you know and the editor will know that the end result is a load of drivel.

I have often managed to produce a half page or even three-quarters of a page of reasonably worthwhile material but from the outset it was always going to fizzle out.

I am now into my second hour trying to find a

worthy subject but I am as far from starting as I was when I first inserted the foolscap into the typewriter.

The mistake I made was inserting the sheet of foolscap in the first place. I am now convinced that if I didn't have to confront it I wouldn't have to deal with it. Now that it's in the typewriter it has me at its mercy. I would feel guilty if I left and went for a walk or a drink.

At least, after thirty-nine years or so, I have learned a very important lesson. I didn't start to type until late in life. The lesson is to leave the foolscap where it is with all the other sheets, not even look at it or the typewriter until the effects of the alcoholic outing have worn off.

There is something challenging and provocative about a blank sheet of foolscap as it looks up at one from the typewriter.

'Fill me!' it seems to say, 'Here I am empty and bare while I might be brimming with sentences that titillate and educate and edify.' A silent typewriter points a finger more accusing than ever was pointed by Kitchener. No half-starved orphan ever presented such a haunting face. To go away and leave it all alone would be an act of desertion without parallel. My only hope is to keep staring it back in the hope that something might come of it and I might end up seeing it filled.

THE DRINKING FIELDS

MEN WHO GROW ANXIOUS for intoxicating drink for reasons which cannot easily be analysed are very often the victims of intolerance and misunderstanding. When I was younger people were more tolerant and when neighbours over-drank you would hear remarks like the following:

'Wisha the poor man is plagued by drought', or 'God help him he's cursed with a terrible tooth for porter'. Those charitable souls of yesteryear never inflicted the hard word when a soft one was admissible.

It must be conceded, however, in these days of affluence, wantonness, permissiveness, etc., that drinking is a more serious problem than ever before and that we should look above and beyond the accepted norms for the root causes of this much-abused practice.

Recent disclosures in the national press about the drinking habits of the Irish people will not have escaped the notice of my readers. That they are true is near enough to fact but a very heavy reduction on the per capita consumption must be allowed on the grounds that we have a large tourist intake not to mention all those buck navvies (of whom I was

once a proud member) who come home annually
and bi-annually and whose recreation time is spent,
in the main, in public houses. For reasons unknown
these navvies and their adherents have never been
regarded as tourists. A probable reason could well
be that they spend too much to be looked upon as
such. I have known many who spent several hundred pounds in the few weeks available to them,
not always on themselves alone but on the many
short-term admirers that a flaithiúil hand can
attract.

I will not go into the reasons given for the Irish
obsession with intoxicating liquor in the most recent published analyses. I have my own theory
about these and I have drawn the conclusion, from
long practical experience, that our heavy drinking
has to do with landscape. Do I hear sniggers?

Let there be sniggers but it should be remembered that I have as much right to put forward my
theories about the causes behind the national
pastime as anybody. Recently I took a break from
the booze. I decided to forego my nightly indul-
gence to honour the memory of a departed parent. I
endured the martyrdom for a month which, when
you make allowance for the resistance of the subject, is a reasonable period of abstention. I might
not have gone back on the stuff for a much longer
period if it had not been for a certain incident
which dampened my fortitude.

I am in the habit most evenings of taking a walk

through a number of boggy fields outside the town. I intrude upon nobody save the occasional snipe who must only benefit from these incursions of mine if he is to be fully alert for the day when fowlers will threaten his very existence.

On this particular afternoon I stopped for a moment or two to savour a few lungfuls of country air. Between breaths I thought I heard a whisper, a sort of subdued, caressing sibilance from somewhere behind me. I looked around but could see nothing. The whispering persisted and shortly I learned that it was coming from everywhere. It was the earth itself and it wasn't whispering. It was drinking. Earlier in the day there had been a number of heavy showers and the noise which sounded so like whispering was the squelchy earth swallowing copious draughts of refreshing rainwater. In short the soggy fields were soaking it up goodo. It was an unmistakable sound and it brought back happy memories of intoxicating beverages which I had so often quaffed myself.

To make a long story short there arose inside me an irrepressible longing for a long and a strong drink of bodied beer in rich quantity to freshen my exhausted fibres and restore to them their old pulpy satiety.

I place the blame fair and squarely on the drinking fields and had it not been for the convivial whispers under the grasses I might have passed on and inflicted further needless tyranny upon my rapidly dehydrating body.

These particular fields are always drinking. Morning, noon and night they absorb moisture. Even in the height of summer they absorb the dews of night and morning and dry as the weather may be they lap up the left-over dampness deep down where the sun can't get at it.

To hear them at their best you would want to pay them a visit after three or four days of heavy rain. Then the noise is almost deafening provided you are prepared to give it your undivided attention. I always say *Sláinte* when I hear these fields indulging thus.

This then could well be one of the undisclosed causes which might explain our predilection for alcoholic beverages to the degree which makes us stand out above other nations. Shakespeare had the same thing to say about Denmark. Correct me if I'm wrong:

> This heavy-headed revel East and West
> Which makes us traduced and taxed of other
>   nations.

I hope that what I have unfolded will be taken seriously. To those who are forever seeking messages I would say that it would be wiser for an alcoholically-inclined person to steer clear of drinking fields and confine himself to the public highway.

IT NEVER RAINS BUT IT POURS

EVER SINCE I WAS a boy I have been fascinated by the pronouncements and conclusions of local weather-forecasters. These men knew their suns and moons, their winds and skies but were modest in the extreme about their accomplishments.

'Tis many a long day now since myself and Mickeen McCarthy borrowed Jack Horan's ass to draw a four-man slean of turf out of Dirha Bog. On our way we met Sir Stafford Cripps and Mr Chamberlain which were the names given to two elderly brothers who dwelt in the farthest in house in the bog.

'Will the day hold fine?' Mickeen asked.

Sir Stafford raised wrinkled eyes to the western horizon and sniffed the wind.

'There's no rain in that,' he said and he turned to the brother for corroboration.

'The crows are flying with their backs to the wind,' Mr Chamberlain announced, 'and by all the powers that be you'll get no rain today.'

The next soul we encountered was Sonny Canavan and he making horse stoolins of dry turf on a bank near the roadway.

'Will the day hold fine?' Mickeen asked.

'Would I be here?' Canavan asked, 'but for I knowing we'll have no break.'

This gave us great heart because the Bally-bunion Pattern Day which is the fifteenth of August was only two days off and Mickeen had a buyer lined up for the turf if we could have it on the side of the road by evening.

'Listen,' said Canavan and he raised a finger for silence. We listened and far away from the west came a sullen deep monotone interspersed with the faint cries of far-off sea gulls.

'What does it signify?' Mickeen asked.

'It signifies,' said Canavan, 'that the sea is near today and when the sea is near you'll see no break.'

Greatly heartened Mickeen produced a paper packet of Woodbines and tendered one each to Canavan and myself. We then sat on our behinds, our backs supported by the stoolins and our legs stretched in front of us, content in the knowledge that we had the day long to handle the job before us. We spoke about the war. The following day Churchill and Roosevelt were to meet at sea. Earlier that year Hess had flown to Scotland.

'If Hess had landed in Dirha instead of Scotland,' said Canavan, 'we'd have an extra man for the slean and we needn't be recruiting townies.'

Earlier that year, as well, the *Bismark*, had been sunk.

'I'll tell ye once and I'll tell ye no more,' said Canavan, 'that Hitler lost his chance. He got his fine days too but he didn't make hay.'

So the conversation went on and on until the shrouded sun began to rise in the noonday sky. We took our leave of Canavan who returned to his stoolins and we made haste for the house of Jack Horan. At either side of the roadway the larks rose singing and the mellow booming of bullfrogs bore witness to the simple joys of bogland life. Now and then a billy goat would raise his head from the herbage to inspect us and mild, summer breezes rustled the tinder-dry heather.

'These are mighty times,' said Mickeen. At Jack Horan's we were greeted by his wife who told us that himself was in bed but that we could have the loan of the ass for five Woodbines. The cigarettes were handed over and we set about tackling up.

'Will it hold fine?' Mickeen asked of Mrs Horan.

'Will it hold fine Jack?' she called through the bedroom window. There was no immediate answer but after a short while Jack Horan emerged in a long night-shirt down to his toes and a cap on his head. There was a cigarette in his mouth. The ass was now tackled and the rail in place.

'Will it hold fine?' asked Mickeen. Jack Horan took the cigarette from his mouth, topped it and carefully placed the butt behind his left ear.

'Look beyond,' he said and he pointed a black-nailed finger towards where the blue mountains of the Dingle range stood out from the background of a clear sky.

'When the wind is from that quarter,' said Jack Horan, 'the weather will stay settled.'

Along the bumpy roadway we walked at either side of the plodding ass. The larks sang louder now and soared exultantly heavenwards leaving behind them wonderful trails of song. Suddenly I was struck on the forehead by a solitary, outsized raindrop. A minute passed and I was struck by another. Then came another and another until it seemed that every raindrop in the sky had specially convened for an all-out assault on Dirha Bog. The rain came down in blinding sheets until streams began to flow at either side of the roadway. The ass slithered and fell and the passage which led to our slean of turf had now become a gurgling stream.

'Never mind,' said Mickeen, 'we still have a smoke left.'

From his pocket he produced a paper packet of Woodbines but, inside, the cigarettes were wet and soggy as bog-mould.

'It was said before,' Mickeen announced, 'but I'll say it again. It never rains but it pours.'

BADGES

WHY IS IT THAT men who wear badges are nearly always the proprietors of sterner and soberer miens than those who wear no badges at all? If you don't believe me look about you. A man of one or more badges will be seen to be less flippant, less fugacious and less feckless than his badge-less contemporaries. Could it be that he is conscious of an added responsibility, that he is aware of a new dimension, that he is the physical embodiment of what the badge stands for or is it because I who am without a badge am self-conscious and, as a result, deferential?

A man wears a badge because he wishes to announce publicly his affiliation to or sympathy with certain organisations and points of view and just as surely as you'll see a badge in favour of one thing you'll see a badge in favour of the opposite except, of course, in the case of those who entertain moderate opinions. Badges, in a sense, are like colours at football matches. There isn't much point in having black if there is no white, in having green if there is no red and so forth and so on. Those who sport colours are expressing pride in their counties or countries and are generally harmless sorts while those who wear no identifying colour are often far more partisan. The same cannot always be said of badges but it is fair to assume that a man who publicly wears a badge has not all that much to hide even if he pretends otherwise.

Do not for a moment get the impression that I am opposed to badges. Far from it. The more the merrier. What worries me is the prospect of too many badges. I tremble at the thought of a personality completely subject to the demands of a badge.

Men wear flowers, shamrocks and palms so why not badges? If all men were equal there would be no need for badges.

A man is easily identified by the badge he wears and while it is not as accurate as an identity tag it tells us a good deal about him, not everything but enough to help us in establishing an attitude towards him. There are some who wear badges at the backs of their lapels rather then the front where everybody can see them. There are a number of reasons why men do this. One of the commoner is that they are at liberty to flash the badge to others who wear it publicly and obviously are in full sympathy with whatever cause it stands for. To those who are opposed to the sentiments expressed by the badge no offence is given because it is not visible. These Tadhg *a' dá thaobh* types have a powerful instinct for survival but often, because they endeavour to keep in with everybody, they have the support of nobody.

Then there are temporary and permanent

badges. For example under the head of permanent might come pioneer pins, Fáinní nua and sean-fháinní, anti-swear pins, blood donor pins, etc., while under the head of temporary might come shamrock sprigs, palms, team emblems, carnations, Easter Lilies, etc. Believe it or not I have seen as many as five of these occupying the same lapel. I have seen a Fáinne Nua, an Easter Lily, a blood donor pin and two shrivelled, decaying remnants of blessed palm and shamrock left over from preceding Holy Days.

A fine thing this, a rare form of loyalty which suggests too a sporting type of fellow who is prepared to stand back from nothing.

We can learn much from men who wear badges which are out of vogue. Let us imagine that the football match is over and that the victory dance is in full swing at a nearby marquee or dancehall. In swaggers a man wearing the colours of the losing team. Now while the sporting of colours may be a fine thing at football matches it can be a highly provocative and dangerous business at dances. Only born agitators wantonly do this. Colours are best left at home when the occasion that originally demanded them is no more.

What of the extended use of the badge? A man who wears an Easter Lily on Easter Sunday does so because he wishes to honour the patriot dead but the man who wears it the following week as well is most likely suffering from delusions of patriotic grandeur and should not be provoked or stared at.

Some people have no need for badges. We can tell by their faces the sentiments that lie underneath. We can gauge from their reactions what force impels them. Small things give them away. A man in love, you might say, is a walking badge. The symptoms are written all over him but only for those who are prepared to take a sympathetic look and I am prompted to ask the question should people who fall in love for the first time be made to wear badges? The answer, of course, is yes although I will not go into all the reasons. One or two will suffice. The wearing of a love badge might remind crusty and intolerant old fogies that they too were in love and it might make us all more tolerant of a disorder from which no one at all is immune.

WHITEWASHER

NOW LET US TAKE a gander at the noble trade of whitewashing. Odd that I should mention the word gander which in this instance means 'look' or 'glance', for you see, dear reader, long before the advent of whitewashing brushes, as we know them, ganders' quills were used for the purpose of laying on the whitewash.

Not everyone, however, is cut out to be a whitewasher. Tall or lanky men simply will not let their ladders work for them as against, for instance, middling-sized or small whitewashers. The long man will insist in extending his limbs above and beyond the limits laid down by the Whitewashing Act of 1925, which emphatically states that no whitewasher 'shall place himself in a position on his ladder which is likely to imperil himself or passers-by'. Remember too that a man leaning too far sideways must, of necessity, compromise his strokes so that blotchy whitewashing is the end result. We, therefore, see that only middling or low-sized men are suited to this particular trade.

When the Whitewashing Act of 1925 was amended in 1927 it took full account of female whitewashers for the first time. As we all know female whitewashers will persist in wearing turbanised headgear of the most colourful kind during operations. Bright scarves and bonnets are also worn on whitewashing occasions. The amendment regarding female headgear clearly states that 'no part thereof shall fall down over the eyes nor shall the pigmentation and arrangement be such that it might serve to attract onlookers into whitewashing areas.' Need I add that this area is fraught with perils.

Physically the ideal whitewasher should be a man of medium size with an easy-going gait, a sound head on his shoulders and an ample belly. He should not be less than thirty-five years of age for the good reason that whitewashing and youthful frivolity do not mix. The ample belly is strictly for anchorage. A light-weight whitewasher is a far more expensive proposition than a heavy-weight or bellied whitewasher. The light-weight will be compelled to hire an assistant to hold the ladder when he is obliged to ascend from the lower rungs to what might be termed dangerous areas at the top of the ladder.

A middling-sized whitewasher with a fulsome belly needs no helper. His ladder will not be easily shifted when his full weight rests upon it. His belly, you might say, is his insurance against disaster. Without it he is prey to every gust and to the assorted mischief-makers of *terra firma*.

No whitewasher is born with a natural belly. The belly is accumulated over the years by means of the easy-going gait mentioned earlier and by the consumption of numerous pints of stout. White-washing is dry work and it's not just because it's fraught with danger that it is dry. Lime which is the basic ingredient of all whitewashes, thick and thin, is a great thirst inducer. Dizziness, which comes from having to scale heights, also induces thirst as does the business of mixing whitewash. The sloshy sounds arising from this activity are noted for the way in which they induce thirst. There are count-less psychological explanations for this which I shall not go into here due to space limitations. Suf-fice it should be to refer readers to two well-known works on the art of whitewashing namely *A White-washer's Childhood* by Eva Brush, the famous North-umbrian cottier, and the lesser known *Recollections of a Bavarian Whitewasher* by Heinrich von der Huernslosher.

There is an opening for a whitewasher in every community. There is a good living to be made and a man is in charge of his own destiny. All that is needed is a head for heights and, of course, a bit of a belly. One important word of advice, however, and this is it. Own your own ladder. Your own ladder is an assurance of a lengthy and trouble-free career. Mounting a strange ladder can be like mounting an unbroken pony or indeed the steed of a stranger. You never know when they'll let you down and to be let down in the world of white-washing is a guarantee of a broken limb at the very least. The most accomplished whitewashers that I recall were small, sad-faced, middle-aged men who took their jobs seriously. The fact that they wore sad faces did not mean that they were sad people. No indeed. They wore sad faces because it had to be seen that their lives were continually at risk. This made it easier for them to charge danger money in addition to their normal day's hire.

I hope that these few observations on the white-washing scene may be of some assistance to the gentle reader. In a world where there is a growing antipathy towards all forms of hard work you know not the hour nor the moment you'll be called upon to do your own whitewashing.

One final note. Whilst it is perfectly acceptable for a whitewasher to consume drink after working hours, it is suicidal to drink during whitewashing. As a career I would strongly recommend it and with jobs growing scarcer every day, it might be the right moment for some unemployed person to make a fresh start in the whitewashing business.

IS THE HOLY GHOST REALLY A KERRYMAN?

IS THE HOLY GHOST really a Kerryman? The obvious answer to this is: If he is not a Kerryman what is he? Is he just another ghost, a mere figment of the imagination like Hamlet's father or Paul Singer's assets, or is he something more sinister; a Corkman masquerading as a Kerryman or worse still a real Kerryman but having an inferiority complex; that is to say a Kerryman who thinks he's only the same as everybody else?

I put it to you now that the question which I am about to pose is the one which holds the true answer. If the Holy Ghost is not a Kerryman can he be the Holy Ghost? The answer of course is no. He cannot. Having established his Kerryhood through theory we are at liberty to proceed so now let us establish it through logic. For this we need attestation, testimony. We need genuine witness. The following true story should be sufficient to dispel any remaining doubts concerning the real source of the spirit in question.

Some years ago one morning during the height of the month of June a young man set out from his home in the perimeter of a bustling city. He turned his face towards Kerry. He was fortunate enough to meet compassionate car drivers on his way so that between the jigs and the reels he found himself in the heel of the evening not far from that awe-inspiring terrain which is known in Kerry as the Conor Pass. In short he was nowhere else but in the seaside village of Castlegregory where the dispenser of his last lift had deposited him.

Here he betook himself to a hostelry where he partook of an egg and onion sandwich and three pints of well-conditioned Guinness' stout. At closing time the barmaid asked him if he had acquired accommodation for the night but he replied that it was his intention to walk the lonesome road to Dingle, it being the month of June and he being in his health.

'But,' said the barmaid who was young and beautiful and concerned, 'you'll have to climb all the ways to the Conor Pass.'

'That,' said the young man with a touch of bravado, 'is my exact intention.' So saying he buckled his knapsack, adjusted it on his shoulders and made for the open door.

'May the Holy Spirit guide you safe,' said the barmaid.

At this the young man scoffed and in that scoff was contained an implicit rejection of the power of the Holy Ghost. With a whistle on his lips the young man set off for the town of Dingle. Mile after mile of road he put behind him until the country-side started to fall away below him and he found himself at the entrance to the Conor Pass, thousands of feet above the level of the sea. Here he slackened his pace for he felt that the worst part of his journey was over. Alas the mountains of Kerry are as unpredictable in temperament as the artists who paint them, the poets who so often extol them and the playwrights who try to portray them.

Suddenly the mist began to thicken on the shoulders of the hills and in a matter of moments the young man couldn't see his hand in front of him. Blindly he groped his way along the narrow roadway knowing that one false step would plunge him into eternity. Inch by inch, foot by foot, he crawled along the road. Then without warning the ground began to slip away beneath his feet and he knew that he had strayed off the beaten path and that his life hung by a thread.

'Oh God,' he shouted, 'Oh God help me.'

There was nothing by way of reply but the sibilance of swirling mists and the whisper of growth deep in the vast tangle of mountain heather. He cried out again and again.

Then in answer to his summons a voice spoke. It spoke in a whisper but it was a whisper of such intensity that it seemed as if all the winds of the world had assembled in that spot to enrich its timbre and deepen its volume.

'Tell me,' said the voice in a Kerry accent, 'are you the man what don't believe in the Holy Ghost?'

The young man made no reply. The power of the mysterious voice had paralysed him. Then a huge and mighty hand, yet shapely, appeared out of the mist and taking one of the young man's hands it led him out of his impasse to where the stars danced in the midsummer sky and a white moon shone brightly on the lonesome road to Dingle.

Well now if that isn't sufficient testimony I don't know what is. From a purely personal stand-point I should inform you that I always invoke the aid of the Holy Spirit before embarking on any work of importance and if I were unexpectedly call-ed upon tomorrow to write an epic poem on sar-dines or sausages I would journey first of all to Ballybunion and thence to its seaweed baths where I would disrobe and submerge myself in the hot sea-water with fronds of glutinous seaweed en-meshing me in their slithery grasp. Then while the Atlantic raged outside I would uncork a bottle of Irish whiskey and indulge in a full-blooded hearty swallow. Up then in my pelt and off in a mad gallop towards the incoming tide. Then when I'm up to my neck in salt-water I would invoke the Holy Ghost:

'Come to my aid oh great spirit. Infuse in me

the white fire of minstrelsy.'

The moral, of course, in the aforementioned is that the poet who does not invoke his muse is a very foolish fellow.

EPITAPHS

Here lie the bones of Pecos Bill,
He always lied
And always will.
He once lied loud
He now lies still.

THE ABOVE WAS ONE of the first epitaphs I ever learned. I heard it on the stage of the Plaza Cinema in Listowel from the lips of a strolling player when I was ten years of age and ever since I have had a hunger for epitaphs of a comic nature. The first original epitaph I ever heard was composed by a local poet named Paddy Drury:

Here lie the bones of Paddy Drury
Owing their size to Guinness' Brewery.

It was never to appear on his headstone which was recently erected at the Old Abbey of Knockanure near Listowel. The reverend mother of the home in Killarney where he died begged him not to allow it to be used so he acceded to her request. My personal choice in epitaphs is that which was devoted to a hanged sheep stealer named Thomas Kemp:

Here lies the body of Thomas Kemp
Who lived by wool and died by hemp.

In second place comes:

> Here lies my wife,
> In earthy mould
> Who when she lived
> Did nought but scold.
> Good friends go softly
> In your walking
> Lest she should wake
> And rise up talking.

For my own epitaph I would not be too choosy. Something simple and catchy like the following:

> Here lie the bones of John B. Keane,
> I hope the grass above is green.
> And when the summer comes around
> May daisies dance upon this ground.

Nothing pretentious. Whatever about the hereafter the most one can hope for in the clay is grass and a daisy or two and, of course, a prayer now and then. I rarely pass by a graveyard if I see one from the roadway but while Ireland abounds in graveyards, quaint, elegant and otherwise the same cannot be said for epitaphs. For such a colourful and humorous people we are notoriously shy when it comes to inscribing our headstones and tombs with writing that is memorable. This is why so few people visit Irish graveyards. In England thousands of visitors call each year to graveyards which have comic inscriptions on their headstones.

There is one honourable exception to the Irish

position and this is the churchyard of Kilfergus in the town of Glin in County Limerick. Here is an outstanding example:

> Erected to the memory of Thos. Pope Hodnett, died Dec. 26th, 1847. They say he was an honest man. Erected by his son Thos. Hodnett, Pastor, Immaculate Conception Church, Chicago.

In the same graveyard which is ever open to passers-by there is perhaps the best-penned epitaph in the country. When I last saw it less than a month ago the characters were as clear as could be on the stone.

> Erected to the memory of Timothy Costello, died June 4th, 1873:

> This is the grave of Timothy Costello
> Who lived and died a right good fellow.
> From his boyhood to life's end
> He was the poor man's faithful friend.
> He fawned before no purse-proud clod.
> He feared none but the living God.
> And never did he do to other
> But what was right to do to brother.
> He loved green Ireland's mountains bold,
> Her verdant vales and abbeys old.
> He loved her music, song and story
> And wept for her long-blighted glory.
> And often did I hear him pray
> That God would end her spoilers' sway.
> To men like him may peace be given
> In this world and in Heaven.

HUMMING

BEFORE COMMENCING THIS STORY I went through considerable soul-searching. My initial idea was to dash off seven or eight hundred words on the subject of humming. Alas I made the fatal mistake of confiding to a friend.

'What about hawing?' he said at once. The remark set me off course. The writing of an essay is a delicate business. One has to be unequivocal and precise. Ambiguity and ambivalence are out. Thus we must agree that a distinction has to be drawn and the question that must be asked is this: 'Can there be humming without hawing?'

Those who combine humming and hawing will hold one view while those who hum without hawing will hold another. My view is that humming is a legitimate and independent transmission of carefully considered inner thought whereas hawing is but a mere part or fraction of a greater whole. For instance one can haw-haw, he-haw and hum-haw but a haw without a hum, a hee or another haw is meaningless and cannot be said to compound a meaningful utterance. Having made this clear we are now free to concern ourselves solely with humming.

Your committed hummer is, of course, a spoiled singer. By committed hummer I mean he who hums whole songs rather than snatches. Your casual hummer is just another man who wants to say no and is merely softening the blow. Then there is the one-note hummer.

He is a man who is asked a simple question but by virtue of a quirky make-up is unable to give a simple answer. He hums away in subdued mono-tone hoping that the person who has asked the question will grow tired and go away. Failing this he silently prays that the listener will deduce some sort of satisfactory answer from the sum of his hums and settle for this in the absence of anything more tangible.

The type of hummer who irritates me most would be best delineated by the following example. Many years ago my mother commissioned a handy man to clean our eaves' shoots. He arrived with a bucket, a ladder and an assistant. Before they start-ed she asked them if they would like a cup of tea. The pair emitted a series of abbreviated but con-formable hums and when questioned a second time treated us with longer and seemingly more thoughtful hums. We deduced that they would in-deed like a cup of tea. In answer to subsequent re-quests such as whether they would like bread and butter, jam, cold meat, etc., they conspired to lead us on with the same disarming hums.

They spent most of the day doing the job and when they finished late in the afternoon I was en-trusted with the task of finding out how much was due to them. I was answered with hums long and short and much serious shaking of heads. This latter was to imply that the amount might be more than usual, when I repeated the question I failed to elicit an answer. All I got was another dose of hums. The going rate per day at the time was ten bob so I asked them if this would be all right. This drew forth a babble of hums, unprecedented in range and depth. In the end we were forced to pay them twelve and six-pence per skull although they said neither yes nor no to any of our offers.

Do not for a moment be so foolish as to believe that this sort of humming is a refuge for the inarticulate. Far from it. Hummers of the type I have mentioned have learned over the years that a meaningless answer can be extremely intimidating. They give the impression that they are being badgered when a simple question is being repeated for the second or third time. The only way to deal with these evasive and demanding types is to hum back at them. It never fails.

Now let us turn our attention to the musical hummer. I had my first taste of musical humming at a 'Feis Cheoil' when I was ten. There was in our class choir a sweet-faced boy who had an equally sweet soprano voice. At the 'Feis Cheoil' he would sing *Danny Boy* and we would back him up with gentle humming.

He got all the credit. We got none. All this went to his head and at one 'Feis' instead of commencing with *O Danny Boy* he started with *O Daniel Boy*. This unexpected grandeur threw us completely and the ensuing humming was a shambles. The boy soprano's voice broke at the same time and so ended my career as a competitive hummer.

If the gentle reader is truly interested in seeking the source of really genuine humming, i.e., humming which is musically expressive and yet linguistically effective, he should ask one of his relatives or friends for the loan of a substantial sum of money.

The answer to such a request is the source of all that is practical and realistic in expressive humming.

DUMP-GULLS

I AM A MAN who loves the seashore. I love the
lapping of small waves as much as I do the thunder
of great ones. I love the ozone and I breathe it in the
way a famished whale savours its first mighty
swallow of plankton. I love the spirit of the sea and
its undying restlessness. Byron speaks for me when
he says in 'Childe Harold':

> Roll on thou deep and dark blue ocean roll.
> Ten thousand fleets sweep over thee in vain.
> Man marks the earth with ruin, his control
> Stops with the shore upon thy watery plain.

I love the awesome power of the storm and I feel in
tune with the seabirds as they wheel and plunge
and soar and drift and glide, loving the strong
wind and using it to hover, dive or climb. Their
cries above the roaring of wind and wave delight
me for these are cries of an ecstasy that man cannot
comprehend. In human speech they would be saying: 'Look at me. I am a bird of the air. I have mas-
tered the wind. I spurn the earth. I know no confines. I am the loveliest of God's created creatures.
Mine is the loveliest of all motions. I outdo ballet in
my grace. I am majestic.'

So well might they boast for they who are
speechless are compensated by the wonderful gift

of flight. I wish I had the space to go on and on and to dwell upon cormorant, guillemot and oyster-catcher to mention but a few of those of our feathered friends who live by the seashore but I have a duty to my readers and so I will deal with what are loosely referred to as seagulls and about one of whom Gerald Griffin had the following to say:

> White bird of the tempest, oh beautiful thing
> With the bosom of snow and the motionless wing.

If Gerald Griffin were to come with me upon one of my daily walks he would not be long in revising his opinion of the seagull. Most of these 'beautiful things' have long ago abandoned the sea for town dumps and places where entrails, trash and other refuse is thrown. Here you will find them in un-believable numbers, these once proud seafarers, squawking and infighting over scraps like hyenas. They have forsaken the glinting cliff faces for the smelly, sickly, ugly dumping grounds of town and city. They rise bleating and shrieking every so often for no reason that is apparent and sometimes they are not above assaulting an innocent pedestrian without provocation of any sort. In winter-time when frost is rife and food is scarce they are not above attacking children and making off with whatever it is that the child happens to be eating at the time. Seagulls my hat. Dump-gulls is a more appropriate name and they should be referred to by this name until such a time as they return to their natural haunts and leave scavenging to the scavengers. I, therefore, propose that we call them henceforth by the name of dump-gull until such a time as they abandon their evil ways and return to their once proud calling as princes of seaside places.

Worst of all I have heard and seen them arguing with common crows. The pandemonium over the snatching of infinitesimal food particles is deafening. No self-respecting seabird should be seen arguing with a crow. Crows are the clowns of the bird world, the rapscallions and the thieves and to be seen in argument with them is a sign of idiocy.

Let me at once absolve the many fine species of gull who have stayed in their native places, who have not been and will not be lured by the easy pickings of town dumps and backyards, proud seamews who have ridden out tempest after tempest and who would mew with disdain at the thought of forsaking their natural habitats for the refuse ground of wingless humans.

It is the dump-gull's squawking to which I most object. It has, in its new confines, reached hysterical proportions and the sad musical beauty of their seashore crying is now no more. Oh what a falling-off there is. There is a lesson for the human here. Do not be in too much of a hurry to forsake your native place for the allure of distant cities or faraway lands. It is better to be king of the mountain and marsh than another digit in another ghetto. Just as the once-noble seabird said goodbye to his natural terrain so too did many fine and noble humans. They swapped the beauty, the simplicity and the frugality of moor and mountain for crowded places to squabble for more and still more until they have become sated with false values and no longer know how to live meaningful lives.

But enough. It is with the seagull that we must concern ourselves and not to forget that he is no longer entitled to that name. He is a dump-gull and will remain a dump-gull until he turns his face to the sea once more.

GARTERS

I AM NOW ABOUT to embark upon a treatise trickier than any I have ever tried before. The subject matter is so potentially explosive and fraught with likely dangers that, in this instance, there may be justification for the use of the Shakespearean adage that 'fools rush in where angels fear to tread'. It was Mark Twain who said that 'man is the only animal who blushes and the only animal with reason to blush'. I hope, however, for another blush, the blush of modesty when I disclose the nature of the subject, i.e., the common elastic garter.

The garter has been in wide use from earliest times but did not come into prominence until the year 1351 when the English King Edward III rebuked a number of onlookers when he, the King, reclaimed a garter from the ground. It had been dropped by the Countess of Salisbury after a dance and when he stooped to pick it up he was so irritated by the suggestive laughter of his courtiers that he was quoted as saying: 'Shame on him who thinks ill of it.'

This led to the founding of the Order of the Garter which should clearly indicate that garters were revered even in medieval times.

There is no Irish equivalent of the Order of the Garter. The first reference to garters in Irish history is to be found in the prophecies of the ancient monks of Ballybunion. These particular prophecies, written in Irish might in fact be referring to the youth of today and I am sure that the ancient monks had this very time in mind when they wrote, in reference to the youth of the future, *Beidh siad gan giobal, cleite no brístín*. Translated into English this means: 'They shall be without garter, plume or knickers.'

We must wait and see whether the monks were wholly right or only partly right. The way things are going it's odds on that they weren't too far wrong.

The monks resided on the Virgin Rock off the rugged cliffs of Doon which stand guard over the golden beaches of Ballybunion. Of the Virgin Rock local legend says this: 'A virgin will not be found within an ass' roar of it till all the seas are still and the tides cease to pour.'

All this, however, is getting us nowhere. The subject is garters and I will now endeavour to adhere to them. At the time of writing the only folk wearing garters are hurlers and footballers not to mention the odd lady who refuses to succumb to tights and still wears pairs of stockings maintained by elastic garters. Referees also wear garters, although many an irate partisan would prefer to see them round their necks rather than their legs.

When I was a garsún garters were all the go and I have lost track of the number of times I was sent to neighbourhood emporiums for yards of black and white elastic ranging from an inch in width to a quarter inch. Older ladies and dowdier ladies would wear gibbles or gibbal, i.e., garters without elastic or if you like any sort of an old cloth which would hold up a pair of stockings. Gibbles were frowned upon by ladies of fashion and it was also common knowledge that they left deep circular welts around the base of the thigh. The fatter the thigh the deeper the welt. Consequently, a lady who was fond of wearing a bathing costume at opportune times had to be very careful about selecting suitable garters. Wide garters left little or no marking on the thigh whereas a narrow garter often bit into tender flesh and left a red band around this most sensitive of areas. Only two kinds of elastic went into the making of garters in provincial Ireland. White elastic was worn by maids and black elastic was worn only by married women and widows, although if certain widows chose to wear white elastic allowance was always made.

The question which arises here is this. Will there be a return to garters? The answer is, of course, yes. There will be a return to garters when women abandon their slavish habits. The trouble with women is when one wears tights they all wear tights but I say to you, as others have said to me, that garters will be as plentiful in my time and yours as was once the moose on the shores of Lake Huron and the midges that swarm under the bowers near the lakes of Killarney.

Garters also played the part of guardian against incursions above the knee. The garter was the timberline of morality and the Plimsoll Line of security. Can the same be said for tights?

THE LOST HEIFER

I REMEMBER A WHITE heifer which was driven to town in the company of two other heifers by a small farmer close on two score years ago. He was forced to sell them because of pure impoverishment. He entered the square of Listowel exhausted and bedraggled after a journey of five hours from the foothills of the Stacks Mountains. It was only seven miles but this was good time when you consider that he had three recalcitrant heifers under his command.

To assist him in this marathon cattle drive he had a ready garsún of twelve or so and a small lean, underfed dog of indeterminate strain. The garsún was his son, a useful lad with his legs, able to move with speed and precision whenever the heifers abandoned the roadway for the familiarity of adjacent fields. No toll much was taken out of the youth. It was the dog and his master who suffered. The dog was never properly trained and whenever he exceeded his duties by misdirecting or snapping at the cattle he fell in for, you guessed it, dog's abuse. The farmer himself was far from being fit. Fear of hunger and overwork left him without the hardiness essential for the successful hustling of heifers over mountainy roads.

The trio of man, boy and dog managed to corral

the heifers in a corner of the square. Here they stood them until jobbers saw fit to inspect them. In transactions of this nature and period it was every man for himself. Backward farmers, unaware of the fluctuation in the market, were often forced to sell cheaply and prematurely rather than be left with cattle on their hands which seldom happened in all truth but there was the danger and it was a trump card the jobber never failed to play.

Our man from the Stacks Mountains had little difficulty in disposing of two of his herd but as the day wore on it seemed less and less likely that he would be able to find a buyer for the white heifer. At the time the farmers of Ireland had little *meas* in white cattle. They were called bawnies and were notoriously slow to develop. Fair-haired or blond people were often nicknamed bawnies when one wanted to imply disparagement.

As the evening wore on our friend would repair now and then to the nearest pub where he would order and consume a medium of stout or maybe two if he chanced to run across an acquaintance. Earlier he had invested in a bag of buns and a bottle of lemonade for the son. Buns were looked upon as luxuries in those days and shown more veneration than fresh meat, sausages or black puddings. In the heel of the evening the dog wandered off after a passing bitch. The youngster, drowsy from the early rising and the long trek of the morning, fell fast asleep where he sat on the kerb. In the pub the boy's father forgot the woes which had ground him down all the year. He swallowed medium after medium of stout until someone reminded him that it would be dark soon and that it would be as gay for him to be chancing the road home. Reluctantly he left the dreamland of sawdust, barrels and bottles and made his way to the corner of the square where he had last seen his heifer, his dog and his son. There was no heifer to be seen. The dog was no great loss. Dogs could be had for the asking but a heifer, even though white, was a different matter altogether. His first act was to wake his offspring. His second was to present him with a box in the ear, this to refresh his memory regarding his last waking impressions of the vanished heifer. The youngster alas had no idea where the animal had strayed. The procedure for dealing with missing cattle in those days always followed a ritualistic pattern. First there was a visit to the guards' barracks where the orderly would promise to do his best to locate the animal. This done the next step was to a central newsagent who would display a description of the strayaway on his front window for a modest sum, generally in the region of a three-penny piece. The next step was the schools. In most towns there was a national school for boys and another for girls. There might also be corresponding secondary schools. The visit to the schools was another day's work and anyway there was always a fair chance that they might encounter the heifer on the way back home. This, however, they failed to do.

The following day the man from the Stacks Mountains mounted his bicycle and headed for the town. It was a wet and windy day but this did not deter him. First he called to the barracks but there was no word there. He tried the boys national school before the others for the simple reason that he had once attended such an establishment himself although without any degree whatsoever of success. He tried each class in turn and ended up in ours which in Oriental parlance might be termed the Class of the Sixth Book.

Here the teacher received him courteously. Then in his own words he gave a description of the heifer: 'She war a narra Bawnie,' he informed us. 'She war stone mad on top of it and she have only a horn and a half.'

Several hands shot up and their owners clamoured for attention. The teacher ignored them. He knew they were only budding Thespians who hungered for the limelight.

When the initial clamour had died the teacher repeated the description. Two hands shot up.

'Where did you see her?' the teacher asked of the first.

'Sir, I can't remember the place but if I was took there I'd remember it.'

'Sit down,' said the teacher. Here, he knew, was a dodger looking for the rest of the day off. The

teacher questioned the second boy who provided
an accurate description of a bohareen where he had
seen the heifer that morning.

The face of the man from the Stacks Mountains
lighted up. When he had first entered the class-
room, wearing his black coat tied with an outsized
safety pin at the throat, he looked like a corpse
with his ashen face and his dark curly hair hanging
wet from under his drenched cap. He carried an
ashplant and his coat was bound round with a
length of homemade hayrope. His dripping trousers
were thrust inside his turned-down wellingtons and
round him, where he stood, pools of water were
forming on the floor.

Looking back now he looked the very per-
sonification of the blighted thirties, a beaten man
but a man who refused to give in. It's no wonder
farmers are doing well today. God owes it to them
from the days of the Economic War and the hungry
years that followed since.

MIXED GRILLS

I HAVE A DREAM. It is to write a thesis on the mixed grill before progress reduces it to an absurdity. This would be the definitive work on the subject. It would be found after Mixed Enterprise (Econ) in *The Encyclopaedia Britannica*. When my name would crop up people would ask what's he done that's so important? There would be a shocked silence from the erudite after which would come the confidential whisper briefly outlining my single achievement. The name Keane would be synonymous with the mixed grill. When I would pass by a crowd people would say reverently and proudly: 'There goes Keane, the mixed grill man.' I would be introduced as Mister Mixed Grill himself. In my obituary notice there would be mention of my most notable achievement. 'Keane was the man,' it would read, 'who rescued the mixed grill from oblivion.' My descendants would come to be known as The Mixed Grill Keanes. That is my dream. I often ask myself if it exceeds my rightful expectations but no answer comes. I believe, however, that it is my destiny. Some men were born to free sewerage pipes, others to pick plums. I was born to write about mixed grills. This is not my first time. I have written several short pieces for radio and newspapers but this is not enough. Once more then into the breach.

Your classic mixed grill, the constituents of which I will disclose shortly, rose to ultimate prominence in this country towards the end of the Second World War. On the same day that the Americans landed in Okinawa another American who happened to be a relation of my mother's landed in Ireland. His first act, after landing, was to make a beeline for the nearest hotel where he ordered a meal for himself and the members of the reception committee. He also allowed the latter to pay their individual parts of the bill, having first graciously declined to accept it himself. My mother was obliged to foot his part of it. It was not a notable occasion. There was no sparkle to the conversation. How could there be with a question-mark hanging over the matter of the bill. There was no wine. In those days wine was offered only at wakes, weddings and christenings. Ordinary people like ourselves required nothing with our meals except pepper, salt and mustard.

I remember to have ordered a mixed grill on the occasion. It is a repast which I remember with affection and respect. What's that Wordsworth said:

> The music in my heart I bore
> Long after it was heard no more.

It consisted of one medium-sized wether chop, two sizeable sausages, four slices of pudding, two black and two white, one back rasher and one streaky, a sheep's kidney, a slice of pig's liver and a large portion of potato chips which were something of a novelty at the time and were, indeed, quite foreign to many parts of the countryside. Accompanying this vast versification of varied victuals was a decent mound of steeped green peas, a large pot of tea and all the bread and butter one could wish for. It was a meal fit for a ploughman and I can proudly recount that not a vestige of any individual item remained on my plate at the close barring the chop bones alone. The total cost of this extraordinary accumulation of edibles was three shillings and sixpence which was the precise amount I had in my pocket. In those days not like now, young gentlemen would know to the nearest half-penny the exact amount of cash on their persons. Tipping in those days, for a chap of my age, was unthinkable.

Since that unforgettable occasion I have demolished more than my share of mixed grills. They were an ideal choice for those who were not prepared to gamble everything on a meal which consisted solely of cold meat or steak or indeed chops be they pork or mutton. If the steak or the chops were tough all was lost whereas in the mixed grill, one could find immediate redress in any of the other constituents individually or collectively.

The mixed grill was, of course, an ideal plate for peckish persons. While none of the ingredients on their own could be described as a substantial course they nevertheless succeeded in substantiating each other. If, for instance, the white pudding was not of the required consistency or if the black was too lardy one could ignore both and still make do with the other members of the confederacy.

The mixed grills greatest single attribute was its variety. All of the ingredients I have mentioned have individual characteristics which set them apart but none is capable of really standing on its own. It is the unification of all the members which gives the mixed grill its strength and intensity not to mention vivacity and colour. Some readers may carp at the fact that I have deliberately not included eggs in the association and in all fairity I should say that authorities are divided as to whether fried eggs should be included or not. I would probably agree that they should but only on condition that a major ingredient such as the liver or the kidney was absent. Traditionally, therefore, all things being in order, your fried egg is purely optional and by virtue of long association has a closer affinity to rashers.

Some of my readers will now be surprised to learn that I have not eaten a mixed grill in over a year. Strange behaviour for a man who has been so generous in his praise of mixed grills. Perhaps, however, not so strange when recent events are taken into account. Early last summer I was on my way home from the capital when I decided to stop at a wayside watering place for a pint of ale. As I sat minding my own business contemplating my diminishing measure my nostrils were assailed by a most appetising smell. I quickly finished my pint and headed for the dining-room where I was presented with a menu. There was such a diversity of foods on offer that I could not make up my mind. I, therefore, ordered a mixed grill. Here is what I got: One apology for a rack chop, two shrivelled sausages, a small wrinkled rasher and an egg more raw than fried. Finally to add to the parody, a writhing mass of badly burned onions. There was also the half of a tomato and two leaves of lettuce which I refuse to take into account. Having no wish to offend the waitress who seemed a decent sort of girl I bolted as much as I could of the mess, paid my bill and said goodbye. I should, of course, have referred the whole business over to Bord Fáilte but I am a tolerant man and decided to refrain from complaining. Maybe the chef had an off-day or a tiff with his wife before starting for work that morning. Who knows what choice error from the vast gallery of human misery attached itself to the poor fellow on that forgettable day.

I haven't eaten a mixed grill since. I have often felt like one but I'm afraid that I will be deceived or disappointed and so I have decided to wait for better times when people will take pride in their work once again and the mixed grill will once more titillate and tantalise those who appreciate its wonders and its subtleties.

BIG WORDS

MOST OF OUR ENGLISH teachers warned us at one time or another of the folly arising from the use of a big word where a small one would do just as well. Be this as it may, however, there was nothing so deflating to an ignoramus or common thug as a barrage of well-timed, well-spaced, multi-syllabic tongue-twisters. Backward and suspicious folk unversed in the subtleties and sonorousness of sublime expression have a healthy respect for the man who has words at will and will give him a wide berth for fear of invoking his wrath. In fact there are many sensible country people who would much prefer a lick of a naked fist.

The worst a belt of this nature can do is give you a black eye or a broken jaw either of which can be cured and forgotten about altogether in the course of time. Not so with a nicely mounted cluster of sharp, scintillating words. These can leave scars and sores that will not heal for a genesis of generations. How many will disagree that an absurd sobriquet has twice the punishing powers of a comprehensive physical beating. The old Gaelic chieftains had a greater fear of satire and ridicule than of sworn enemies out for a man's blood. At least you could build castles against your enemies but against the invective of a disgruntled bard there was no defence whatsoever and even if you cut off his head before he got started one of his brotherhood was sure to lambast you with a lacerating and lineage-defiling displode which was sure to be remembered unto the third and even the fourth generation.

Anything was preferable to the poet's curse or the wit's tag and if 'twas the last forkful of meat in the house itself it was wiser to part with it rather than risk the wrath of a starving poetaster.

Worse still, of course, was to be fettered by a mouthful of words which the benighted victim would have no hope of understanding. Bad as he is the devil one knows is better than the devil one does not know and what an ordeal to have to go through the world like a dog with a canister tied to its tail.

There are others, of course, notably schoolboys, who have no fear whatsoever of the spoken word when delivered by a disgruntled teacher. The longer the tirade the less likelihood of physical punishment. The maxim here was:

Sticks and stones may break my bones,
But words will never hurt me.

However, I remember a singular exception to this. Many years ago in Listowel there was a secondary teacher by the name of Paddy Breen who was reputed to be one of the best English scholars in

Kerry. Once after an argument with an inspector he was asked by the school's president to render an account of what happened.

'All that happened,' said Paddy, 'was that I bade the fellow beat an ignominious retreat to the native valleys of his own obscurity.'

There was in Paddy Breen's heyday a pupil attending the school who arrived each morning unfailingly late. Always he would come up with a different excuse. It so happened that one morning Paddy was taking the first class of the day. Our friend, as was his wont, arrived a half hour late.

'Well,' said Paddy, 'what excuse have you to offer this time?'

'My mother's watch sir she stopped,' was the inventive answer. All the other clocks and watches in the house had long since been rendered inoperable due to a variety of misfortunes.

'You sir,' said Paddy Breen, 'are the misbegotten metamorphosis of a miscalculating microchronometer.'

Our young friend took the jibe poorly and did not attend class the following day nor indeed for many a day afterwards. Eventually Paddy received a solicitor's letter asking him if he would be good enough to repeat the damaging statement in court. Paddy replied that he would be agreeable and sent the solicitor an exact copy of what he said. No more was heard of the matter but had he used smaller and more easily understood words there would have been no misunderstanding whatsoever. Alas there would have been no colour either and the class would have been a drabber, duller place. Readers then may gather that I do not altogether agree with teachers who lay too much stress on simplicity. All the words in the dictionary are there to be used and every word no matter how discum-bumbulating it may be deserves an airing now an then. A sameness of small or undistinguished words will definitely present a practical and clear picture but they will not alas present a memorable picture with, of course, the honourable exceptions such as Four Ducks in a Pond and the like of which only serve to prove my point.

HEIFER COURSING

MY SOLE AIM IN compiling this story is to create employment where none existed before which brings me now to the métier of the sports organiser, on a professional basis, I need hardly add. Since cities, towns and other built-up areas are well-catered for in this respect we must look to the countryside. There are many lucrative openings in this field and a young man with energy to spare and a modest amount of capital to invest can look forward confidently to success.

Let me, therefore, endeavour to establish my aspirant in his chosen career. Here is how he might begin. First let him invest in a score of mountainy heifers, the leaner and wilder the better. Isolate these temporarily in an out-of-the-way pasture and, at his leisure, prepare an advertisement for the newspapers. Let it state that there is to be a heifer-coursing contest for thirty-two farmers in the heavy-weight class. Light or agile farmers would not serve our purpose as you shall see.

Let there be an entrance fee of say £100 per farmer which would give him purse and expenses money of £3,200. Let him present £1,500 to the winner, £500 to the runner-up and to the beaten semi-finalists £250 each. This leaves £700 for advertising, insurance and the salaries of the organiser and his assistant or assistants. Allowing that there would be an admission fee of a pound or two the afore-mentioned sum would more than pay for the hire of the venue and for the remuneration of the judges.

First let there be an open draw to select sixteen pairs of farmers. When this is done the heifers should be brought down from the hills or wherever to the venue.

Let the coursing then commence – two farmers to chase one heifer which would have roughly a hundred yards start. The idea would be to award points to the farmer who succeeded in roping the heifer taking into account first, second and third turns as in greyhound coursing. After the first round we would be left with sixteen fitter and faster, less weighty farmers. There would be no public outcry as in greyhound coursing. Indeed the organiser would be more likely to be commended for providing the district with fitter farmers. Abulia, inertia and obesity would soon disappear from the face of the countryside and there would be a greater interest in fitness on the farmlands in general.

However, let me return to the second round of the heifer coursing. By this time the lazier and fatter farmers would be weeded out but amongst them there would be a resolve to do better in the next heifer coursing contest. Indeed there might be a consolation stake for sixteen no-course duffers.

The main contest, however, would go on until all have been eliminated save for the two finalists. Imagine the excitement as the fastest of the heifers, specially confined for the final, is released. The last two farmers are slipped and off they go after the heifer amid wild cheering from the crowd. They swing their ropes and emit ancient and traditional cattle calls as they endeavour to capture the heifer. Afterwards the cup is filled and the loser congratulates the winner in a sporting fashion.

The sports organiser then moves on to the next venue where a similar event would take place. The winners of local contests would go forward to compete in regional contests and from there to the national final.

The most attractive aspect of heifer coursing is that anybody can enter. As well as that an essential service is being provided. Overweight sons of the soil who cannot be induced into Turkish baths or weight-losing establishments have at last been presented with a means of losing weight and not only can they lose weight but they can gain glory.

Heifer coursing need not necessarily be confined to farmers. City people, however, who might be frightened of cattle might avail themselves of cats or even dogs which could be pursued over specially laid-out courses which might have obstacles like water trenches or hurdles.

You can see, therefore, that there are immense possibilities in heifer coursing for heavy farmers.

People might abandon their armchairs for a while to spend some time in the healthy outdoors and heaven knows how many new jobs would be created. Government aid from the Department of Health should readily be forthcoming. A fit farmer must, of necessity, produce more than an unfit farmer. A government subsidy, therefore, would be a wise investment and would yield a fine harvest in time.

There are, of course, numerous other forms of sport which might be utilised for the good of the country. In selecting heifer coursing we have shown that new jobs can be provided without affecting other job sources. We have shown that the most vital ingredient of all for creating new employment is the imagination. Indeed the imagination, because it is not fettered by strictures, should be used more and more by industrialists, politicians and job-planners in general.

If heifer coursing does not appeal to you you will always find something that will if you put your mind to it, by simply using the imagination the good God has given you.

CREAKY STEPS

THERE USED TO BE a creaky step on the stairs of the house where I was born and reared. As an alarm system it was without equal and no matter how carefully one trod on it, it always reacted noisily.

It was a step for which I had no love but nothing would induce my father or mother to have it repaired.

'That step,' said my father, 'always informs me of the homecoming hours of my sons.'

It was indeed a third party. It was also a traitorous double-crossing slat of timber which creaked ominously and often cockily when one of us was out longer than he should.

We used to try avoiding it but somehow it succeeded in passing on the information to the next step which creaked informatively, no matter how light one's footfall. This led me to believe, and I have no reason since to doubt it, that all stairs, great and small are possessed of this single traitorous step.

My father was proud of our step. In his eyes the other steps in the flight were common fellows not worthy of notice. Years afterwards when we had grown up and gone our separate ways in the world he still cherished the step and refused to replace it and events proved he was right for the step was to fulfil a role similar to that played by the Capitol geese when they saved Rome or Killorglin's puck goat when he forewarned his friends and neighbours of approaching invaders.

It was the second night of Listowel Races and my mother and he were fast asleep. Night is not quite correct since it was two o'clock in the morning but you know how people say night when they really mean morning. For instance the song: 'Who were you with last night?' should I have no doubt, read: 'Who were you with this morning?' If the girl in question was home before twelve, the song would not have been written. Nobody minds a girl having a night out but a morning out is a different matter.

But where was I?

Yes, it was two o'clock in the morning and my father was snoring away to his heart's content. He was, as snorers go, in a class of his own. In this respect the Tonic Solfa held no terrors for him and he cavorted between high do and low do like an apprentice operatic singer.

Sound asleep as he was, when the step creaked he awoke immediately and seized a poker which he always kept handy. He did not go out on the stairs but called out from the safety of the room.

'Who's there?' he shouted.

No answer at first but when the step creaked again he knew that the invader was at least intimidated and contemplating retreat. My father waited a few moments and then went out on the landing, clutching the poker. He was, it is only fair to say, followed by my mother.

'There's nobody there!' she said.

'Correction!' said my father; 'you mean there's nobody there now!'

'Maybe 'twas the cat?' my mother suggested.

'Nonsense!' said my father. 'No cat could cause a creak like that.'

Months later, when we were all at home for Christmas he told us about the incident. He gave a description of the intruder. 'The scoundrel must have weighed fifteen or sixteen stone,' he said. 'He was also remarkably fit, either a wrestler or a fighter.' My father deduced all this from the two creaks. 'But for that step,' he concluded, 'we would all have been murdered in our beds.'

'There was only the two of us in the house!' said my mother.

'When I said "all of us" I meant the two of us,' my father announced.

The following night, St Stephen's Night, the step betrayed us individually and collectively as we entered at all hours from dances and parties. My father didn't really mind the time but he liked to know what was going on.

I have on my own stairs a similar step and sometimes, when I go to football matches, the missus says: 'If I'm asleep when you come back, don't wake me up!' I promise I will do this and always I keep my promise. But one night the step creaked and she woke up. I spent the next two hours describing the match. In the end she asked; 'What woke me?' I told her it was a creaky step. 'Nonsense,' she said. 'We have no creaky step.' I left the room and told her to listen. When I came up to the step in question it creaked in a most objectionable manner. When I returned to the room, she was satisfied.

'You know ... ,' she said, before she went to sleep.

'What's that?' I asked.

'Nothing,' she said, 'but it's just that I've always wanted a creaking step in the house.'

I like the step myself because it is more than likely that it will be an asset to me, the same as my father's was to him. A creaking step is as good as a dog and it eats very little – just a fragment of wax-polish now and then.

CANAVAN'S DOG

IT MUST BE FIVE or six years now since I last made mention of Canavan's talking dog, Banana the Sixth. In response to numerous letters from readers over this period I am happy to assure them that all is well with this remarkable canine. Banana is now in his tenth year and from time to time is given to those priceless utterances which have made him justly famous. The other night as he and Canavan sat by the fire the dog's attention was caught by a report which appeared on the back page of a paper which Canavan happened to be reading. He placed one of his paws on the column and indicated to Canavan that he would appreciate it if the contents of the report were read out to him. Canavan obliged. The dog, as everybody knows, is illiterate although a fluent speaker in both Irish and English. At the head of the column was a photograph of a man and a dog and this was what claimed Banana's interest.

It transpired that the report was an obituary notice on the famous American conman, Joseph Yellow-Kid Weill. The dog was one of Weill's internationally known talking dogs although people who purchased the dogs claimed that immediately afterwards the mutts were permanently stricken with laryngitis. This may have been true to some extent since Weill was a competent ventriloquist.

Canavan's dog nodded his head and wagged his tail when his master concluded, a sure sign that he was about to make a major pronouncement which he promptly did.

'That dog,' said he indicating the one with Weill, 'is a cousin of mine.'

'How can that be?' Canavan asked, 'when none of your seed or breed was ever in America?'

'My dear man,' said the dog, 'my late ancestor, Banana the First, had a sister called Spot who was press-ganged aboard a rat-infested coffin-ship for the sole purpose of disposing of the rats in question. She never returned to her native Lyreacrompane because nobody would give her a passage home to the Land of Slugs and Dossers. Instead of dying of a broken heart which any ordinary bitch would have done she instead mated herself to a one-eyed Yukonian watchdog who was three-eighths wolf, one-eighth Alsatian, one-eighth Elkhound and three-eighths Kerry Blue. Of issue there was but one male who went on to father the only known American family of talking dogs. This dog, therefore, which you see before you is a blood cousin of mine. Need I say more.'

'Fair enough,' said Canavan, knowing that it was useless arguing with the dog when he struck a vein like this. The pair sat silently in front of the fire watching the flames as they flickered in the ancient hearth. Outside a curlew called and in the distance a dog barked. Deep in the bog a lost ass brayed long and low and a mating bittern bleated romantically.

'You referred there,' said Canavan, 'to the land of Slugs and Dossers when you must have meant the land of Saints and Scholars.'

'Slugs and Dossers is what I said,' Banana the Sixth announced firmly, 'and Slugs and Dossers is what I meant. Is it a country where men who won't work and who were used only to ass and carts ten years ago have now fine motor-cars? Is it a country where men earning several thousand pounds a year are looking for more when old-age pensioners are expected to live on a fraction of that? Looking for more imagine and they having plenty already. Is it a country where they won't show up for work and where doctors' certs are as common as bogwater?'

'Now, now,' said Canavan, 'you'll give us a pain so you will.'

'Don't mind your now, now,' said Banana the Sixth, 'don't you see them yourself resting in their motor-cars and they reading when they should be working? Don't you see them at everything except the job they're getting paid to do? There is no work being done in this country at the present time. Don't I see them going down that very road outside to the bog and they wearing low shoes and collars and ties. What country could stick that kind of carry-on? It couldn't last. No country could carry so many dodgers and survive for long. A nation of

Slugs and Dossers is what I said and a nation of Slugs and Dossers is what I meant.'

So saying the dog rose and went out into the haggard where he addressed himself to the moon which was in the last quarter. He howled high and clear until a band of ragged clouds came from the direction of Ballybunion and hid Diana in their midst. The dog went indoors and sat in his favourite place near the hearth. Canavan put out the lights and went to bed.

BOHAREENS

Oh, I do like to wander down the old bohareen
When the hawthorn blossoms are in bloom ...

(Song)

ONE OF THE GREAT tragedies of this modern age is that people do not go walking down bohareens any more.

They don't walk up bohareens either, because one must go down to come up.

The dictionary has words for those who explore caves and collect coins, but there is no word for the bohareen-walker. All around us are little roads and grass-covered, rutted tracks that lead to nowhere. There should be a society for the preservation of bohareens or, if this is not possible, each of us who have an interest in what is simple and good in life should adopt a bohareen. Nothing could be less expensive for all that has to be done is to repulse take-over bids from companies like Briars and Nettles and Thistles and Docks and to encourage small businesses like the Wild Rose and the Buttercup.

Walking down bohareens is a must for those who find members of the opposite sex endearing and a man who hasn't walked down a bohareen with his best girl has missed much. Those couples who haven't held hands and skipped a bit between high whitethorn hedges had better do so at once, not for my sake but for their own. Who knows what woes will taint the winds of coming summers and, after all, we're only young once. Now is the time and who knows better than those of us who dallied with sweethearts of yesterday that we are travelling on a one-way ticket in this topsy-turvy world and truly the man who has paid his dues to bohareens can say when his hair, if any, is grey: for me the past has no regrets for I am one who has honoured the little roads that lead to nowhere.

I myself have not given up bohareen-walking and I know a few good ones where children can be nurtured to appreciation, where the only traffic is the annual hay-car and the only life the occasional donkey without portfolio. The bohareen is the last sanctuary of over-worked ponies absent without leave, rogue nanny-goats, hare-shy greyhounds, indisposed hedgehogs and other unseen creatures who prefer the cloistered quiet of grassy ways to the tumult of terror-laden thoroughfares.

The bohareen is a refuge, a haven for harried souls who like to amble along safe from the noisome jarring of car horns and the sudden death that their absence precipitates. This is the age of racing, because people are always in a hurry these days and I doubt if many know where they are really going. They're burning it up and those of you who

speed like lunatics through the fear-filled countryside would be well advised to slow down when
you're passing the hallowed entrance to a bohareen. You would be wise to stop and stroll down.
The heady scents and peaceful surroundings might
steady you down and, who knows, the half-hour
you should spend there might not be the cause of
saving your life but it could be the cause of saving
somebody else's.

I don't know what put bonnets into my head
but the setting for a flowery bonnet is a bohareen, a
background of browsing cows and woodbine wild.

Nobody thinks more of the bohareen than he
who has no access to it. Many a man in New York,
Durban or London would give his right hand to
saunter down the distant bohareens of his boyhood
and the woman who wrote the 'Old Bog Road' was
one whose heart was in the right place or, if you
like, in her native bohareen.

The bohareen is the by-way of the uncom-
mercial traveller. It is absolutely rustic and the man
who pollutes its purity with the exhaust-fumes of
an obstreperous motorbike is guilty of sacrilege to
say the least. Even bicycles should be barred and
nothing but what is truly conservative admitted to
its protective windings. A small chuckling stream
may accompany it but this is not really necessary
either, so long as there is no scarcity of sheltering
whitethorns and an adequate disorder of all that is

wild in flowers. Nowhere does the bee buzz so soothingly and even the bandit wasp is respectful in such sacred precincts.

Blackberries and elderberries thrive and it is a poor bohareen that doesn't lead to shining sloe groves and mushroom-dotted pastures. Instead of a gin and tonic I would be inclined to saunter down a bohareen to assuage the pangs of hangovers and sick heads. I have never visited a psychiatrist. Why should I when I can go to a bohareen for nothing and figure myself out at my ease?

You don't need an umbrella or a plastic coat if your choice of walk favours the bohareen. You can stretch yourself back against a mattress-like hedge and relax under a canopy of mixed leaves. The fragrance of crushed herbs will delight you while the rain hammers the open roads and drenches the green fields.

It is rather strange that those who mass-produce attractive picture-postcards should show a somewhat prejudiced preference for ungainly cliffs and unsporting seas. I have never seen a picture postcard depicting a genuine Irish bohareen but still, despite all forms of neglect and the absence of any sort of National Bohareen Protective Society, the tiny uncharted lanes of tousled greenery have lost none of their charm and still remain unspoiled and unobtrusive.

Some time, if you have little else to do when

you visit a great city, you may see a prosperous elderly man leaning across the parapet of a bridge. Do not disturb him if you are looking for the nearest way to the theatre. He is remembering evenings of long, long ago and wishing that he was back again walking the bohareens of his green years.

> Had I my chance to journey back, or own a King's abode
> 'Tis soon I'd see the hawthorn tree down the Old Bog Road.

MORNING SOCIALS

LOOKING OUT OF MY window the other morning, I beheld two middle-aged women with message-bags.

The bag of one held cabbage and potatoes. There was also a bloodstained brown-paper parcel which contained either chops, steak, or boiling beef. The message-bag of the other carried cabbage and potatoes also but the meat looked like bacon. The parcel was neater, without bloodstains and it is my belief that there may have been a pound and a half of good quality bacon involved.

The women conversed for some time. The face of one grew serious and perturbed when the other disclosed certain facts. Fingers wagged as much as tongues and the other woman who had been listening took up the running. Time ticked on and the Convent clock struck eleven.

'I'll be killed!' said one, but she made no move to leave.

'They'll be out from school,' said the other but instead of departing she launched into another story. There was some laughter, some sighing, some headshaking and there was a marked coolness when a third woman with a message-bag joined them. Here, I told myself, are three people from three separate walks of life. Here, I told myself, are three cooks, three mothers, three wives. Here are three citizens, three voters, three television-viewers. They're all these things, I told myself and yet they're women too. They are engaged in women's conversation. This is hallowed ground and no man may enter.

I ask myself what was so unusual about the little gathering but could not find the answer. A fourth woman joined the party and they talked on. They shifted a little now and then to make way for other pedestrians. They all stopped talking occasionally to acknowledge the salute of a passer-by. They smiled and immediately their faces became serious again as news of import circulated. Further up the street, on the other side, three other women stood in a group. In the distance it could be seen from the nodding of their heads and the eloquence of their hands that news was being swapped. Directly underneath me the talk went on. I could not hear a word of what was being said nor did I want to. I tried to fathom the causes of such conversations and in the end I got it.

These informal street-gatherings are what pubs are to men. These are social get-togethers, unadvertised but not accidental.

Occasionally a phrase did come across, such as: 'They say it cost twenty pounds!' or 'He don't like it fat!' One particular phrase which recurred consistently was: 'I'll be killed!' Each of the women said this from time to time as if it were a ritual. The phrase intrigued me but it was not, I knew, to be taken at face value.

Every woman who participates in the pre-dinner parley is obliged to say it now and then. It means that she is rushing the conversation, that she is afraid enough will not be disclosed in the time left at her disposal. I often heard my own wife say it while she stood in the doorway exchanging views with a friend. When the conversation dragged, she would say: 'I'll be killed!' I myself the innocent party without malice, not to mind murder, would listen to this and know that the conversation was only beginning.

Beneath me, the four women changed their message-bags from one hand to the other. One put hers on the ground and re-adjusted her headscarf. 'I'll be killed!' she said and listened eagerly to what another woman was saying.

If I had been truly chivalrous I would have located a tray and sent it into the street with four cups of coffee and a plate of biscuits. I fear, however, that my kindness might be taken for sarcasm and while I do not mind incurring the wrath of my fellows, I draw the line at a gathering of four basking housewives.

Hardly fifteen minutes had elapsed since the meeting had begun. The woman with the cabbage, potatoes, and the bacon seemed to be the chairman. Now and then she acknowledged a point of order and gave short shrift to unsubstantiated contributions.

Finally she brought her gavel to bear on the message-bag and concluded the proceedings with the following satisfying summary: "Tis all hours of the morning, I'll be killed!'

TROTTERS

THE UNUSUAL HOLDS A fascination for everybody but if only we were prepared to reflect we would discover that what we believe to be unusual is quite common-place and, in fact, deserves no mention at all. Take for example those numerous parents who see in their own children the embodiment of all that is unique, beautiful, and talented and who see nothing at all in the child next door who may have ten times the talent and ability. Old carpers who are fond of knocking these treatises of mine will ask 'what's he at now?'

Patience, dear readers, and you shall see. It must be plain to all that I will shortly be writing about some thing or body which is unusual, which, in short, is well worthy of the comments I propose to make.

I was present some months ago at a football game. I was one of many hundreds who had come to pass away an hour or so watching a sport dear to us all. The teams took the field after the usual delay and after a brief inspection plus a short lecture by the referee the whistle was blown and the game was on. It started at a cracking pace and there were several minutes of unbroken play which had the crowd on their toes and the majority cheering wildly for one side or the other. It is at moments like these when all eyes are fixed on the commonplace that mine are drawn away to look for the unusual. It is a good time for people are somewhat uninhibited and behaviour is truly normal.

There was nothing exceptional about the crowd or about the wheeling seagulls overhead. The elements themselves were as normal as they might be for the time of year. My eyes were about to return to the field of play when they were arrested by a movement at the other side of the field. It was the linesman dashing to and fro. He was never still and was the antithesis of our own linesmen who never left the same position lest his enjoyment of the game be interrupted. He was one of those experienced and cunning officials who sees the ball go over the line but does absolutely nothing except wait to see how the majority of the players behave. If the majority move downfield he will indicate with his flag that the free is to be downfield and vice versa if the majority move upfield. If there is the slightest contention he will throw in the ball himself. Before we begin to despise this type of linesman let us remember that he is in favour of majority rule although some of the majority may come from sideline support. But to press on; the linesman at the opposite side was a tireless fellow and extremely conscientious to boot. He was the epitome of vigilance, a quality, incidentally, for which sideline men receive more abuse than thanks.

Looking at him stirred my memory and it occurred to me that his behaviour was different from
all other linesmen I had seen over the years. I could
not quite make out what it was that made him
different but different he was and there could be no
doubt about that. I watched him more closely and,
ever anxious to improve the mind and add to the
store of knowledge, I waited till half-time when he
came across to our side.

It was only then that it dawned on me what he
was. It took time but there could be no mistaking
that lifting of the leg, that kick of the feet when he
made haste and finally, conclusively that way he
held his head in the air.

This man was a trotter. In stature he was small
as almost all trotters are. In addition, his legs were
short and if devastating proof were needed, which
it isn't, his posterior was very near the ground.

In short, he had all the classic points of the true
trotter. Incidentally, trotters are very rare. The
world is full of gallopers and trudgers but the trotter is so rare that one could spend an entire lifetime
without meeting one.

After the match he trotted towards the exit.
Notice I say trotted and not walked. Many there
were who walked and some there were who ran
but only he of all who were there was prepared to
trot.

When I say he trotted I do not wish to imply
that he was in a hurry or that he moved faster than

most. He moved at a pace which was just a trifle faster than a good walk. All the time the head was held high and all the time his pace was even. Outside the ground he trotted towards his car and as he opened the door I could almost swear I heard a whinny in the far distance beyond our yesterdays.

I haven't seen a trotter since but I am always on the look-out for one. Be on the look-out for a man with the points I have noted and one day you, too, may see a real, live trotter.

GREAT GOALKEEPERS OF OUR TIME

MONUMENTS ARE NEVER ERECTED to the type of man I have in mind. His words are never quoted and his opinion rarely sought. His greatest quality is his abundance. He forms the majority. He is ninety-nine per cent of any crowd and you can almost be certain that he will never be interviewed on a television programme. When he dies only a few will mourn him, but that is hardly the point, for this man has made his contribution and that, in itself, is worthy of mention.

But perhaps my picture is not too easily recognisable so I will try to draw the man accurately – and the only way to do that is to create a situation.

First of all, take any given Sunday in summer-time. He gets out of bed. He shaves. He dons his sportscoat, flannel pants, and sandals and goes downstairs to a breakfast which inevitably consists of a rasher, an egg and a sausage. He is not feeling too well but he puts the breakfast where it belongs all the same. He glances through the papers and goes to Mass. He doesn't go too far up the church but he doesn't stand at the door either. After Mass he stands at the nearest corner for a few minutes. He meets a man just like himself. There may be certain physical differences but they are two of a kind. A stranger looking on would be at pains to observe any sort of communication between the two but, by some colossal instinct which defies analysis, they enter a nearby public-house together.

In the public-house the customers are talking about a football match. The local team are playing in a challenge game in a village several miles away. Our man goes home to his dinner of roast beef, peas and potatoes. He has a good stroke with a knife and fork and is no joke when it comes to making the spuds disappear. After dinner he is between two minds – whether to go to bed or take out his bicycle and go to the football match. The stout and the heavy meal have made him drowsy but the instinct of the sportsman is strong within him. An uncle of his was once a substitute for the North Kerry Juniors and a cousin of his mother's was suspended for abusing a referee.

Our hero duly arrives at the football pitch. The crowd is small as this is a game of little consequence. He parks his bicycle and pays a shilling admission fee. The teams are taking the field. His interest is aroused. He gives vent to a spirited yell in support of his own team. The familiar jerseys have brought his loyalty to the surface but he notices a discrepancy in the side. He counts only fourteen men and then, suddenly, he hears his name being called. The first faint suspicion dawns on him but he pretends he doesn't hear. Casually he begins to saunter to the other end of the field but the voice, pursuing him, grows louder. He increases his gait but the unmistakable call arrests him:

'Hi Patcheen! Will you stand in goals?'

He can run away now and be forever disgraced in the eyes of his neighbours, or he can stand and be disgraced anyway. His coat is whipped off and, before he knows it, there is a jersey being pulled over his head. He hears a disparaging comment from some onlookers on the sideline:

'Good God! Look what they have in goals?'

His blood is up. He thrusts his trousers inside his socks and tightens his shoelaces. He takes up his position and the game is on.

He is not called upon to do anything during the first half or during the second half either. There is little between the teams but what little there is stands in favour of our man's team. A high lobbing ball drops into the square. The backs keep the forwards at bay and our man goes for the ball. He gets it – only barely but the important thing is that he gets it. The forwards are in on top of him. He's down. He holds on to the ball like a drowning man and for the excellent reason that he has nothing else to hold on to. He hears a rending sound. His flannel trousers are torn. One of the shoes is pulled off his foot. Someone has a hold on his tie and is trying to choke him. He is kicked in the shin and he receives a treacherous wallop in the eye. There must be a hundred men on top of him!

Then the whistle sounds and he is able to breathe freely. He is safe now and here, at last, is the great opportunity. He rises with the ball in his hands. He hops it defiantly and then, in one of those great moments which only happen once in a lifetime, he goes soloing down the field. The whistle blows again but he pretends not to hear it. Then he stops and turns and with a tremendous kick aims the ball straight at the referee. Dignified, he returns to his goals with his torn flannels flapping behind him and his tie sticking out from the back of his neck like a pennant on the lance of a crusader.

Nobody offers him a lift after the game. He cycles home to his supper of cold beef and bread and butter. He changes his clothes and makes no attempt to conceal the black eye. He combs his hair and walks down to the corner. He meets his pal and they stroll leisurely towards the public-house.

Our man calls for two pints and, settling himself comfortably on his stool, launches into a detailed account of the save. If he adds a little it is understandable – and if he had been wearing togs and boots heaven only knows what would have happened. The important thing is that he wasn't found wanting when his time came. He made no headlines but he didn't disgrace himself either. The football scribes will not mention him when the annals of the great are being compiled but in the eyes of his compeers and in consideration of the porter he had drunk and of the dinner he had eaten I think he must surely be reckoned among the great goalkeepers of our time.

MATCHMAKER

RECENTLY A YOUNG MAN came to me in search of a job, any kind of job, his own words. Alas there were no jobs available as I found out when I tried to help him. To be more accurate I should say that there were no orthodox jobs available. I suggest, therefore, to today's crop of unemployed that they create their own openings. For instance there is no matchmaker operating in Kerry at the time of writing.

There certainly is a need for one. I can testify to this. There's no week I don't receive a visitor questing a long-term partner and there's hardly a day I don't receive a letter asking me to intervene in man's constant struggle with loneliness. Unfortunately, I have neither the time nor the talent to be of genuine assistance but I would be prepared to forward correspondence on the subject to a genuine matchmaker.

Dan Paddy Andy O'Sullivan was the last matchmaker to operate in Kerry. From his modest home in Renagown, Lyreacrompane he conducted a flourishing trade and was responsible for directing four hundred couples to the altar of God. He had only one failure out of the four hundred and that was when the female member of one particular contract decided she was prepared to fulfil every role required to her save that of bedmate. No marriage can survive under such conditions so the couple separated. It wasn't really Dan's fault but he accepted responsibility nevertheless.

So where does all this preamble leave us? It leaves us with a vacancy for a matchmaker. To any man willing to fill the role I can guarantee success. The secret is to charge enough. The demand is there as anyone in the Kingdom of Kerry will tell you, as indeed anyone will tell you from Malin Head to Cape Clear, from Canberra to Newfoundland.

Dan Paddy Andy made many a wise and many a prophetic statement during his sojourn in this vale of tears. The most memorable and prophetic that I recall is the following and it has particular reference to what I said earlier about young men making their own openings.

'You may make hay,' said Dan, 'while the sun shines and you may stoke your turf when the wind blows but as sure as there's mate on the shin of a wren there's more to be made working the head at the shady side of a ditch on a wet day.'

Ah what foresight is here, what astuteness! In the tersest of terms Dan tells us that the obvious way is not always the right way. While ordinary men laboured at ordinary chores Dan examined unexplored territory.

As he once said to a television producer during the shooting of a film about matchmaking when asked if he felt nervous about appearing on television: 'No,' said Dan, 'for I'm a man who would knock on every door to earn a bob.'

And Dan did knock on every door. He even built a dance hall in the wilds. No doubt he plotted this one out at the shady side of his beloved ditch while the rain drove relentlessly through the glens and ravines of the Stack mountains. Remember that the only alternative for Dan was emigration. I can see him as though it were yesterday, fingering the rigid stubble in his resolute jaw as he devised ways and means to support his family. I daresay it was out of sheer desperation that the idea of becoming a matchmaker came to him. A man without a shilling in his pocket or the filling of his pipe will resort to quare measures and while Dan's certainly were not quare they were unorthodox.

Dan's great achievement was staying at home in his own countryside with the wife and family he cherished. All around him men and women were packing up and leaving, bolting and nailing their doors and windows and departing for England or America, most of them never to return. Dan stuck it out. His methods of earning the requisite bobs for survival met with criticism from laity and clergy alike but there must have been a lot of truth in the old saying that God loves a trier. Dan survived. You might say, in fact, that he succeeded.

This is why it is so important for young men to repair to the shady side of the ditch or the privacy of their own rooms or indeed to the toilet. The late

Robert Leslie Boland in his fine poem 'Ode to a Lavatory' describes that little, snug spot as 'the throne room of soliloquy', which indeed it is.

In these unlikely, out of the way places, a man may contemplate upon his future with the coolness and detachment which that unknown quantity so richly deserves. It was in such a place that the great matchmaker Dan Paddy Andy O' Sullivan after much self-examination made up his mind to be a matchmaker. It was a historic decision. He left his mark upon the countryside. Indeed I wrote a book about him in Irish entitled *Dan Pheaidí Aindí* which turned out to be a best seller. The matchmaking supplemented the income from his small farm and from his tiny dance hall.

I would ask those who are jobless to consider the life and times of Dan Paddy Andy. Never was there likelier fodder for the emigrant ship. Remember too that he was nearly blind. If you cannot find an orthodox job look around you the way Dan Paddy Andy did. Create you own opening. I know for a fact that there is no full-time matchmaker operating in this country just now so why not be a matchmaker and guarantee yourself fame and fortune.

CORNER-BOYS

TO BE A CORNER-BOY one must be fit for nothing else. It is a career into which men are born, not thrust. A corner-boy can, in his own time, become an institution.

Nobody loves a corner-boy, not even other corner-boys, so how, the gentle reader might well ask, can it be called a career?

It was a wise man who said that as long as we have corners we will have corner-boys. We are, therefore as it were, stuck with them. They have become part of the fabric of our society although some unkind observers are likely to maintain that they belong to the outer edges of the fabric or to that part which is more frayed than the rest.

This is not so. We have had corners since the very dawn of civilisation. Therefore, we have had corner-boys since the very dawn of civilisation. They have established themselves through long tradition which is more than can be said for those drop-outs who simply stayed at home. Corner-boying is a career, without material reward maybe, but a career nevertheless.

Indeed, it might be said that as surely as faith without good works is dead, so also a corner without a boy is dead. There is nothing sadder than a corner-boy without a corner. There are others who have searched in vain for the right corner and never found it. A corner-boy takes one look at a corner and he knows instinctively that this is the corner where he wants to spend the rest of his days.

It may be occupied by other corner-boys at the time but then it is a poor corner that can only accommodate one boy. Most corners maintain two, three, four and even more. As a rule, however, there is only one constant corner-boy. Others come and go and are no more than part-time corner-boys but your resident corner-boy never deserts his post unless he is forced to do so by circumstances outside his control.

He has, as indeed we all have, his natural enemy. The writer's is indifference, the thatcher's is stormy weather and the sea captain's is fog. The corner-boy's is rain. He can withstand hail, snow and storm but not rain. Snowflakes can be brushed away. Hail rolls off harmlessly, but rain penetrates and so he must abandon his post through no fault of his own. On really wet days you won't see any corner-boys. Make a point the next rainy day you're out of doors to examine the corners you pass. You're more likely to see a polar bear than a corner-boy.

Some years ago I had a conversation with a corner-boy of my acquaintance. As a rule, corner-boys are not conversationalists. They are listeners. By virtue of their exposed positions they are prey to passers-by. If these happen to be loquacious or simple-minded or merely drunken people the corner-boy is forced to lend his ear to the musings, ramblings and general verbal output of his tormentors. He must do this or vacate his position. Only the years bring him immunity and in time an amused smile is his only reaction to whatever he is told.

The conversation I had was unique in that it afforded me the deepest possible insight into the mind of a corner-boy. It was, as I recall, a dull afternoon in mid-winter. I had intended going for a walk but the skies had an intimidating look about them. I could well be letting myself in for a comprehensive drenching I told myself. I crossed the road and stood irresolutely at the corner, asking myself would I go or would I stay.

'Quiet today,' I threw the question at the corner-boy in residence. He did not reply. He produced a cigarette box, extracted a cigarette, the sole occupant of the box in question. He put the cigarette in his mouth and deliberately threw the box on to the roadway.

This was an old ploy. He had several such boxes in his pockets, each containing more than one cigarette. If he produced a box containing more than one cigarette he might be expected to part to other corner-boys or to acquaintances in the immediate vicinity. The next thing he produced was a match which he lighted by scraping it against the wall at his rear.

Then he spoke. 'It's always quiet,' he said, 'I'm here thirty years, man and boy. I've never seen it otherwise.'

I was pleasantly surprised that he answered. I knew him to be man of few words. I had at best expected a grunt of agreement. I decided to press my advantage. Here was a man of the outdoors, a man who might be versed in the vagaries of the weather.

'Do you think it will rain?' I asked. He looked upward and cogitated. His gaze remained riveted to the sky for a long period, during which time he consistently wetted his lips with his tongue and thrice drew deeply on his cigarette. Then he answered:

'Hard to say,' he said.

'The forecast says it will,' I told him. He scoffed and spat, topped his cigarette and quenched the glowing ash with the sole of his right shoe.

'Forecasts,' he scoffed again. 'Yesterday they promised bright spells and if you had binoculars you wouldn't find the blue of a child's eye in the sky. As for the day before. You remember the day before?' I nodded eagerly, not wishing to interfere with his recollections.

'They promised us a ridge of high pressure.' He was laughing now. 'A ridge of high pressure they said and what did we get? I'll tell you what we got. We got a downpour.'

'Do you remember Neddy Connor?' I asked, entering into the spirit of the thing.

'I do indeed. Why wouldn't I remember him. Wasn't he related to my mother. There's a man could forecast the weather. He had a nose for rain. He reminded me of nothing but a pointer the way he'd cock that nose, warts and all, into the wind.

'Thunder he'd say and you have thunder fit to burst your eardrums. Snow he'd say and before the day was out the roofs of the houses would be white. Rain he'd say and, by God, you got rain.'

'He was some forecaster,' I said, 'and that's a fact about his being able to smell rain.'

'Rain,' he spat out the word derisively. 'Who the hell wants rain anyway?'

'Farmers,' I suggested. He scoffed at the mention of farmers. Let me say here that he was a natural scoffer. Every single scoff was more pronounced than the one before. They were mocking, ironical and sarcastic.

'Anglers,' I said. 'Anglers want rain.' I said it to provide him with material for another scoff. The scoff came, more pronounced and effective than its predecessor.

'Fruit growers,' I suggested. He had no sympathy for fruit growers either. 'Then you have ducks,' I said. 'Duck always want rain.'

There followed an unprintable exclamation.

'Nearly everyone wants rain,' I said.

'Well, I don't. I don't want the damned thing,' he shot back. 'In fact, the last thing I want in this world is rain.'

'But there has to be rain,' I reminded him.

'Who says so?' he asked aggressively.

'Everybody.'

'Not me. I don't want it.'

'But if you have no rain,' I told him, 'everything will wither up.'

'I'm the opposite,' he said. 'Rain withers me up.'

'How could rain wither anyone?' I asked.

'When it rains,' he explained passionately, 'I have to go home. There's nobody at home. There's always somebody here. I'm happy here. At home I just sit and wait for the rain to pass. The longer it takes to pass the more I wither. Let it rain by night. I don't mind it raining by night. Let it rain any time except when I'm standing at this corner.'

I was quite unprepared for his tirade against rain. I have presented his sentiments as best I can recall them. He looked quite exhausted after holding forth. He looked upward and muttered an imprecation. He had no buttons on his coat but he drew it together symbolically, indicating that he was about to depart.

He pulled up his coat collar and suddenly like a frightened coot he crossed the road and disappeared around a corner further up the street. A raindrop struck me on the forehead. Another did likewise. In no time at all the skies opened up and the rain came down in earnest.

I hurried indoors and surveyed the dismal

scene through my front window. The corner was deserted, but I had a better understanding of the denizens who frequent it. The corner-boy had said but little, but in that little there was much. In a few words he had explained his case. *Vir sapit qui pauca loquitur.*

WATERY EYES

PEOPLE WHO WEAR LONELY faces are not necessarily lonesome people. Much the same applies to people who have watery eyes. We tend to think that these are teary eyes. The truth is that tears and eye-water come from two different fountains. Do not ask me where these fountains are situated. All I can tell you is that they are in the neighbourhood of the noodle. Go to your doctor if you want exact information but don't tell him I sent you.

Watery eyes are just about the most priceless possession a man or woman can have in this little globular demesne of ours. Since, unfortunately, it is a demesne where hypocrisy is more abundant than charity watery eyes can be greatly undervalued by those who are lucky enough to possess them. I myself do not possess watery eyes except when there is a strong wind blowing into my face or on rarer occasions when I am the victim of a head cold.

My ancestors, however, were not deficient in the matter of eye-water and there was one particularly vicious relative who had a good word for nobody but who was greatly liked and respected by his neighbours. They said that in spite of his scurrilous tongue he had great nature. Nature, in those days, was a thing no sensible man should be without. A man with nature, whatever else he might not have, was always accorded respect and if ever his neighbours were heard to criticise him someone was always quick to point out that for all his faults he had great nature. This generally nipped the criticism in the bud.

Anyway this relative of mine was a great man for attending funerals. The only reason he went to funerals was to pass away the time. He did not like plays or pictures and besides you had to pay good money before you were left inside the door of a playhouse or cinema. Funerals cost nothing and he never failed to express his delight when he heard somebody was dead. He had as little time for the dead as he had for the living. Ordinary people who were fond of criticising a deceased party when he was alive always stopped the practice when he was pronounced dead.

There were two reasons for this. A dead man was harmless and therefore praise couldn't do him any good. Number two the louder the praise given at the dead man's wake the greater the quantity of strong drink given to the bestower of the praise.

But to get back to my relative. On the morning of the funeral he would shave and dress in his Sunday best. Always he would make his way to the front of the funeral where he would be seen by all the relatives of the deceased. He always walked with his head well bent and his hands behind his back. This sort of posture impressed everybody.

At the gate of the churchyard he would precede

the coffin party to the grave and stand watching all those who came to pay their respects. Those who did not know him often mistook him for a detective.

At the graveside his eyes would begin to water. He could not keep it back and it often ran down the side of his face. He would produce his handkerchief and blow his nose. Then he would wipe the water away. I once heard a woman behind me say to another: 'God bless that man but he has woeful nature.'

As the water coursed down his face others who were at the graveside, particularly middle-aged women who were in no way related to the dead man, would sniff at the sight of him. These sniffs were the harbingers of genuine salt tears. They would look at my relative again, and believing him to be genuinely crying, would start off themselves. Soon every woman at the graveside was crying. They could not stop even if they had wanted to. Handkerchiefs appeared by the score and eyes were dried only to fill again from the inexhaustible well of tears owned by every woman. If there was a fresh breeze his eyes would really swim and very often sympathetic souls would come forward and place the hand of consolation on his shoulder.

When he died he had a large funeral. It was dominated by women. All had plentiful supply of handkerchiefs but they were never called upon to use them. Not a tear was shed because they had no-

body to lead them. Their tear-leader was no more
and he who was the cause of so many was buried
without a single tear in the end.

DIRECTION-GIVER

I WILL NOW LOOK at the vocation of direction-giving. To be a fully qualified direction-giver one must spend several years as a corner-boy. In point of fact it must be said before we go any further that direction-giving is the only promotion available to corner-boys, which is, after all, a pleasant and un-demanding job whereas direction-giving calls for alertness and courtesy, two qualities missing from the make-up of most corner-boys. In spite of the fact that it is the ultimate in promotion as far as corner-boys are concerned there is no extra remu-neration. Both the corner-boy and the direction-giver are supported by the state. That is to say they are provided with the dole by a grateful govern-ment and while this is no more than enough to keep body and soul together your direction-giver will be the first person to tell you that he is not in it for the money.

Although direction-giving is absolutely male-dominated, no attempts at infiltration have so far been made by women. The same applies to the position of corner-boy. There is no immediate ex-planation for this unless it is that a woman standing at a corner might easily be mistaken for a member of the oldest profession in the world.

At the corner across the road from this humble

residence there is a direction-giver in attendance most week-days. I remember when he was an ordinary corner-boy, one of several who support the corner in question.

In those days there was nothing about him to suggest that he was a putative direction-giver. Like his colleagues he studiously ignored all those who lowered their car windows to enquire after the right road to Ballylongford or Ballybunion. When passers-by stopped to find the location of a house in the neighbourhood he imparted the knowledge with the greatest reluctance and often he simply ignored the unfortunate enquirer. Thus was he showing that he was no moonlighter. He was purely and simply a corner-boy and nothing more and nothing less than a corner-boy.

One day, out of the blue, the most unlikely member of this corner-boy fraternity stepped boldly and resolutely forth when a car driver lowered his window to enquire after the road to Abbeyfeale. Our friend did not answer at once although he might have. The directions to Abbeyfeale are of the most elementary nature.

Instead he digested the question with great care before dispensing the directions. He also placed his left hand on his right hip and cleared his throat. I knew at once that I was watching a newly-ordained direction-giver in action. Having thoroughly digested the question he scratched his jaw with his right hand and puckered up his mouth. He then

removed his left hand from his hip and with a
delightful flourish swept an imaginary lock from
his forehead. Having thus disposed of the imaginary lock he spoke rapidly and pointed decisively
in the direction of Abbeyfeale.

Then with a deprecatory display which involved both hands he brushed aside the profuse
thanks which the driver of the car tendered. He
permitted himself the barest flicker of a smile but
there was a look on his face which seemed to say
'Virtue is its own reward,' and that, after all, is
what direction-giving is all about. If your sole interest in a job is the monetary aspect read no further but if you really seek satisfying, self-rewarding
employment read on. If you are in search of a
career which will benefit your fellows, stay with us
and perhaps we may be the cause of directing you
towards a vocation, outside the common mould.

A qualifying pre-requisite, perhaps the most
important, is a thorough knowledge of the sur-
rounding countryside and a familiarity with
houses, lanes and streets in the more immediate
neighbourhood. Secondly one must have a pleasing
appearance and while nattiness in dress is not essential, it will do no harm if one is careful about
one's attire.

Forelock-touching is not expected but a respectful attitude is to be commended nevertheless.
When disclosing directions one should never over-
elaborate. Provide the information required but no

more. Then withdraw respectfully to your corner to await the next lost soul.

Direction-giving, let me state here, is the sort of job which ensures sound sleep at night. The conscience is clear. Individuals and families which might have otherwise gone astray have been placed firmly on the right roads. The old and the infirm have been re-united with their loved ones. Misguided commercial travellers have been successfully re-routed and hapless wayfarers might have wandered erroneously *ad infinitum* were it not for the succour rendered by the direction-giver. As they say in the more sonorous tongue of the ancient Romans, *Virtus Sola* or as we intimated earlier, virtue alone ennobles, so let us leave things at that and be content.

CAREER AVOIDANCE OFFICER

I HAVE SHOWN IN my selection of unorthodox and unusual careers so far that there are numerous openings into new modes of employment and that no person need be unemployed if that person has shown a willingness to follow the instructions.

Now I will treat with the most intriguing career of all and that is how to avoid a career and still survive comfortably. Career avoidance courses, as far as I know, have not been previously dealt with in the general run of publications to be found in newsagents and bookstores. Time, therefore, a start was made.

Let me begin with the obvious if for no other purpose than for getting it out of the way so that I might explore the less obvious.

A man who wishes to live a life of ease and comfort very often marries a working woman who is prepared to support him through thick and thin, in sickness and in health, etcetera.

Almost always he is a man of good looks, charm, poise and elegance. He is witty, urbane, eloquent and, of course, broke. Believe it or not there are women who will support this type of career avoider all the days of their lives. All they want in return is the fellow's love. This he is prepared to grant in moderate doses in return for his keep and the handling of any surplus monies which might become available from time to time.

There are many such companionable liaisons and while passionate or lyrical love is rarely if ever provided by our career avoider there is a blessed absence of that bickering and quarrelling which is to be found in so many seemingly successful marriages. Here then is a man who has made an outstanding success of his life through the most elementary method of career avoidance. Now to the less obvious.

I am of the belief that where you have extremely large families provision should be made for one career avoidance officer. We have all heard of the outcast members of large families referred to as black sheep or a black ewe but surely a male outcast should be labelled a black ram. Our career avoidance officer, however, is far from being a black ram. He is generally a gentle, easy-going fellow who makes no attempt to fend for himself. By properly executing this simple technique he earns the sympathy of the more progressive members of the family. He lets it be seen by all that he simply cannot make out on his own. Let me call my subject Jack.

'Ah poor Jack!' they will say as though he had never properly grown up and needed constant care. If Jack is prepared to work his loaf a little he may find himself spending Christmas with one sister and Easter with another, part of the summer with another member of the family and the other parts with other members. If they are a worthwhile family they will surely provide him with some sort of a home and occasional unconditional gifts to supplement the meagre dole money provided by the state. Unmarried members of the family might be induced to remember him in their wills. Occasionally and inevitably efforts will be made to find a soft job for poor Jack. The knack of avoiding all forms of employment no matter how soft is not easily acquired.

Jack, of course, will be a past master at the art of keeping work at bay. He can throw a fit, mental or physical or both. He can disappear for a period and return bedraggled, exhausted and unkempt or he can resort to the age-old, simple pain in the back. The back is the prairie of the anatomy. Here are maladies of every description, impossible to isolate because of the vastness of the area under scrutiny. All one has to do is point a finger backward over the shoulder, vaguely indicating the area under stress. Under no circumstances should an exact place be specified. The doctor may have doubts but he will always give the benefit of that same doubt to the patient.

Another sure method of career avoidance is to make a mess of any job you are likely to be offered in the early stages of your life. No matter how easy it is to do it right, always make certain you do it wrong. In no time at all you will acquire a reputation for being a butter-fingers or even a dunderhead. Prospective employers will avoid you like the plague and you are irrevocably launched on a work-free career safe from kind-hearted employers who are prepared to give a willing soul an even break.

Deafness is another useful ploy. The career avoidance candidate should hear only what he wants to hear. He should ignore all forms of instruction which might be to the advantage of his employers.

He might also keep his workmates entertained or otherwise stimulated so that concentration on their tasks is made impossible. His aim at all times should be to undermine any sort of constructive approach to the job in hand. Initiating needless strikes is another stratagem which will not endear him to his employers. I could go on and on but my purpose is simply to show that there are many untapped sources for career avoidance. If we go by the premise that it takes all kinds to make a world there should be a modest proportion of career avoidance persons in every community. It is an interesting way of life. There will be criticism and there will be comment of a derogatory nature as a matter of course from those who work on a regular basis but there is the undoubted compensation of sitting on the sideline while others do all the work.

A HIGH MEADOW

John B. Keane

Mollie's face clouded as it always did whenever she thought of the Ram of God. She was careful not to show her annoyance. The more she considered their relationship the more her fury mounted. She was always fond of saying that there was a fly in every ointment no matter how settled the scene. There was always one hitch and the Ram of God was hers. Somehow, in the course of time, she would bring him down. There was no doubt whatsoever about that in her mind. She would use the man by her side and his powerful connections, unknown to either, but use them she would in the pursuance of her steely determination to ruin the one man who had so far proved to be invincible as far as Mollie was concerned. She would find a way. She tried in vain to subjugate the intense annoyance which the mention of his name always seemed to stimulate ... 'I'll even the score with the Ram of God and he'll rue the day he crossed swords with Mollie Cronane.'